The Italy Conspiracy

J. D. Mallinson

ISBN: 1-4564-8194-0
ISBN-13: 9781456481940

Inspector Mason mysteries:

Danube Stations
The File on John Ormond

chapter 1

"How's your German these days? Chief Inspector Harrington asked George Mason at their routine morning conference in his well-appointed office at New Scotland Yard.

It was a bright day in late spring, when the first flowers were coming into bloom in the gardens below the second-floor window and sporadic birdsong faintly penetrated the double-glazing.

"A bit rusty," Inspector Mason replied, warily. "Haven't used it for several years."

"But it came in quite handy on that trip you made down the Danube a few years back, as I recall," Harrington observed, pouring himself a tot of his favorite whisky without offering it.

George Mason sighed wistfully, as river scenes from that epic journey suddenly crowded his mind.

"What exactly do you have in mind? he enquired, sensing that something more than linguistics was involved.

"Something crossed my desk last week that may be just your line of country," the senior officer said, "in view of your excellent record on foreign assignments."

"I'm listening," Mason replied, with an air of anticipation.

"We've had a tip-off through Interpol regarding a se-ries of thefts of rare books from university libraries, mainly in Switzerland, Italy and southern Germany."

"What kind of tip-off?" asked Mason, dubiously.

"It actually emerged from a plea bargain," Harrington explained. "A Dutch dealer in antiquarian books and rare music manuscripts, known as signatures, has been indicted with fencing stolen goods. In return for a lesser charge, he has offered information about sources, one of which may lead back to the English community in Zurich."

"*May* lead back?" quizzed Mason.

"That's what I said," Harrington replied, with a hint of impatience.

"A bit vague, isn't it?"

"Afraid so. I was approached by the Swiss police, to see if Special Branch could be of some assistance to them. Naturally I thought of you, in view of your previous record. I take it you have no objections?"

George Mason recognized that at once as a rhetorical question. His personal feelings on any police matter were completely beside the point. If his chief had ear-marked him to go to Zurich, he had better starting brushing up his German, and the sooner the better.

"But why would the Swiss want us to get involved? Surely, it's their territory."

"They want to conduct a very low-key investigation, at least at first. The Dutch lead may not be wholly reliable and in any case is rather vague. Leutnant Rolf Kubler—that's the person you'll liaise with when you get there—thinks that a Special Branch agent could much more easily insin-uate himself into the English community than one of his own men could. Moreover, since you're overdue a spot of leave, I thought you might welcome it as a change from rou-tine matters here. Think of it as a kind of holiday and find out what you can. If nothing turns up, we'll write it off as a false lead. No harm done."

"So what you're really offering me is a kind of working holiday?"

"You'll need some sort of cover," Harrington said, side-stepping the veiled reproach, while recharging his glass from a bottle of Glenfiddich he kept in a drawer of his desk. "So I've come up with your new profession. Introduce yourself as an agent for Bowland Tours who is vetting suitable venues for guided tours by bus from England."

"Bowland Tours?" quizzed Mason, intrigued at this unexpected streak of ingenuity on the part of his normally staid, matter-of-fact superior.

"Operating out of Clitheroe, Lancashire."

"And how do I penetrate this English community?" Mason wanted to know, beginning to warm to the project.

"According to Leutnant Kubler…"

"*Loitnant* Kubler," Mason interposed, correcting the pronunciation.

"Much obliged," said Harrington, stiffly. "You always were adept at languages. According to Kubler, one focal point is St Wilfrid's Community Church near the Kunsthaus art gallery. Sunday morning service begins at 10.00 a.m. It's based loosely on Anglican rites—*The Book of Common Prayer*—but is, in fact, interdenominational. In addition to that, there's a theater group founded by novelist James Joyce in the nineteen-thirties. They stage contemporary English and American plays."

"Think I'll stick with the church," Mason said. "Amateur dramatics isn't really my thing, but I have sung a fair bass in church choirs before now."

"Excellent," boomed Harrington, rising from his desk to peer across Whitehall. "You'll manage just fine. All you need now are the titles of the missing books."

He returned to his desk, drew out a small folder from the top drawer and passed it to Mason, who immediately opened it.

"No need to go through them all now," Harrington said. "You'll have plenty of time on the plane to brief yourself."

Mason contented himself with a quick appraisal of the first two items.

"*The History of Westminster Abbey* by Randolph Ackerman," he read aloud. "First edition. Estimated value 12,000 euros."

"It's the hand-painted plates of both interior and exterior views that create most of the value," his chief explained. "It went missing from the Walter Klein Bibliothek at the University of Konstanz."

"And what do we have here?" Mason enquired.

"That's an even rarer item," Harrington explained, leaning forward across the desk for a closer look. "Palladio's *Architettura*, in the original Italian. From the early 18th Century. Again, it's the illustrations that give it exceptional value."

"Over two hundred copper-engraved plates? No wonder it's valued at 30,000 euros."

"And sorely missed by the Academia Enzo Fulgoni at Luino, in whose possession it has been since 1750. There's even a reward for its return. 5000 euros."

"Luino?" quizzed Mason.

"A small market town on the shores of Lake Maggiore, in northern Italy."

"Suppose I vet it for a Bowland tour?"

"Don't stretch the expense account too far," his chief cautioned. "Our budget is limited. Let the Swiss police do most of the leg-work After all, it's *we* who are assisting *them*, rather than the other way round."

George Mason replaced the documents in the folder, which he then put in his briefcase before rising to take his leave.

"We've booked you a flight from Heathrow in three days' time. Should be enough to straighten your affairs here. Collect your ticket and initial expense allowance from Administration on your way out. Transfers of funds will be made bi-weekly to the Kantonal Bank on the Bahnhofstrasse. You'll just have to produce ID. Keep in touch by telephone from your hotel."

"Will do," agreed Mason, from the doorway.

"Good luck and bon voyage."

It was a little past midday when George Mason stepped out into the bright sunlight of the Bahnhofplatz, having caught the morning flight from Heathrow to Kloten Airport and the connecting train to the Hauptbahnhof, Zurich's main railway station. It was a busy scene, with taxis pulling up outside the main entrance and blue, two-car trams snaking their way in and out of the large tram interchange to his left. Pedestrians jay-walked through the busy motor traffic in the direction of Bahnhofstrasse, the city's main street. Gulls wheeled overhead, keeping close to the river. Enquiring of a traffic warden the way to the Niederdorf, he grabbed his suitcase and crossed the bridge over the Limmat, to reach the Limmatquai on the other side. Directly behind the quai and parallel to it ran the Niederdorf, which he followed past fascinating shops selling jewelry, artwork and wood-crafts; small cinemas and nightclubs; Italian and Swiss restaurants, sandwich bars and a host of other amenities that would come even more vibrantly to life after dark. About half-way along, he located Hotel Fiedler and checked in, with the feeling of being in the very heart of this fascinating city.

Shown to his room on the second floor, he tested the bed and unpacked his belongings before freshening himself up in the neatly-appointed bathroom. Crossing to the window, he had a good view of the Niederdorf and river behind it, through a gap in the buildings opposite. Church spires with large painted clocks filled out the elegant sky-line; motor launches plied to and fro ferrying early tourists; pedestrians milled in the narrow street below him, closed to traffic. The detective was well pleased with his new surroundings. His room was cheerful, with tasteful modern décor, and ideally situated to his purposes. He arranged his effects neatly in the drawers and wardrobes, calculating that he had time for a light lunch before his meeting with Leutnant Rolf Kubler scheduled for 2.00 p.m. at the Polizei Dienst.

Locking his room door behind him, he slipped out of the hotel and followed a short side-street past L'Escargot, a small restaurant emitting the aroma of snails roasted in garlic butter. Not quite his thing, he considered, as he gained the Limmat embankment and found an open-air establishment right on the water, where he could watch the river traffic and the gulls wheeling overhead. He ordered *salade nicoise* and, as he waited, his eye took in the succession of bridges leading up to the river's point of exit from the large lake reaching down to Rapperswil. Each bridge had its own character, flanked at either end by church steeples or what appeared to be official government buildings. Zurich Cathedral, the mother church of the Swiss Reformation with its unmistakable twin spires in Romanesque style, dominated the scene. The French salad, one of his all-time favorite dishes, was most appetising. Afterwards, he ordered coffee and lit a small cigar, while perusing the street-plan he had obtained at Kloten Airport. The Polizei Dienst, he discovered, was located just behind the Hauptbahnhof, at most a fifteen-minute walk in this compact city.

Leutnant Kubler was expecting him.

"So glad you could make it," he said, showing the detective into his office overlooking a secluded area of parkland, fringed with mature beeches.

Kubler was rather short in stature, with close-cropped hair and horn-rimmed spectacles. He cut a dapper figure in his dark-blue service uniform with rank insignia. Age about fifty, Mason estimated.

"Had a good trip out?" he enquired. "Hotel satisfactory?"

The detective nodded affirmatively, easing his large frame into the chair offered him.

"Couldn't ask for better," he observed.

"Let me know at once if you have any cause for concern," Kubler said, helpfully, "and we'll look into it right away. Now, to the business in hand." He shuffled some loose papers on his desk and put them aside, peering closely at his visitor.

"The theft of rare books," Mason began.

"Chief Inspector Harrington has already given you a briefing, I understand. What we need is for someone to infiltrate the English community to see if he can turn up some useful leads. This business has been going on for quite some time and, frankly, my superiors are not well pleased that so little progress has been made in getting to the bottom of it."

"Breathing down your neck?" enquired Mason, sympathetically.

"You could put it like that," Kubler said, with an ironic smile. "The truth is, we don't have a great deal to go off. The stolen items have simply vanished."

"Into private collections, most likely, in the Far East and North America."

"At an educated guess, yes," the lieutenant conceded.

"But why an English connection?" Mason wanted to know.

"A Dutch dealer in antiquarian books and manuscripts, who has confessed to the Amsterdam police that he has occasionally fenced stolen property, slipped out a reference to a St Wilfrid's, then quickly retracted it. They suspect his motive was fear. Nothing, not even a lighter prison sentence as part of a plea bargain, could persuade him to elaborate further. He's not, by the way, implicated in the current series of thefts. Just grapevine gossip, I suspect."

"So?"

"The Amsterdam people have checked all possible links to the name Wilfrid and its German equivalent, Wilfried throughout western Europe, including universities, cathedrals and parish churches, specialist libraries, societies and so forth. They came up with several possible candidates, one of which is St Wilfrid's Community Church, right here in Zurich."

"A pretty slim lead," Mason countered, thinking to himself that at least, thanks to Harrington, he would get some sort of vacation time out of it.

"I sincerely hope you don't think we are wasting your valuable time," Kubler said, half apologetically, his eyebrows raised.

"Not in the least," his visitor replied, expansively. "Zurich is a beautiful city. It will be my pleasure to get to know it better."

"We really are most grateful," the other said. "It may mean something or it may mean nothing. But an Englishman such as yourself would be much better placed than one of my own men to penetrate that community, which consists mainly of English-speakers. Not necessarily all Britons. Americans too, I believe."

"An international affair, then. Adds to the interest. But tell me, Herr Leutnant, at this stage have you any idea what sort of people may be involved in these book thefts? Are you thinking of a lone agent, or possibly an organization of some description?"

The lieutenant stroked his chin and thought for a moment, his brows knit in concentration.

"Rolf, by the way, is my first name," he said, after a while.

"Mine's George," Mason responded, genially.

"Impossible to say for now," Kubler said, reverting to the original question. "An individual is certainly not ruled out. And the term 'organization' can cover any amount of mischief. Did you have in mind, perhaps, a terrorist organization?"

"Not necessarily," Mason replied. "Although such groups are quite active at this point in time."

"In Britain, certainly, as in other parts of Europe," the other agreed. "I appreciate your problems in that regard. But they're not particularly evident in Switzerland."

"Except perhaps in financial circles," Mason wryly observed.

The lieutenant gave a fleeting, rather sardonic smile, but let the jibe pass.

"Many groups operate across national frontiers," Mason continued.

"Baader-Meinhof and the Red Brigade are long past. But of course there could be others starting up which have so far kept a fairly low profile. Animal rights groups, anti-globalists, environmentalists. You name it, there's a group for it."

"A fact of modern police life," his visitor said, resign-edly. "No rest for the wicked." Rolf Kubler smiled to himself at that remark, sensing a degree of kinship with the uncon-ventional detective opposite him. He then drew from his drawer a sheet of paper which he passed across the desk.

"This is the latest reported theft," he remarked, con-cernedly.

Mason perused it thoughtfully.

"*The Old Man and the Sea*", he exclaimed. "Valued at 25,000 euros? Isn't that rather a lot of money for one of Hemingway's shorter novels?"

"It's extremely rare, in fact," Kubler explained, "being one of the few copies actually signed by Hemingway late in life, when he had grown more reclusive and did fewer sign-ings and interviews. Many consider it his finest work."

"I can believe that.," Mason said. "Read it myself some years back. It's a gripping tale, comparable in some ways to *Moby Dick*." With that, he withdrew from his briefcase the file Harrington had given him and added this latest item to it.

"In the event that you may need back-up," the lieuten-ant then explained, "for routine investigative work…"

"Leg-work, you mean?" Mason quickly interposed.

"Exactly," Kubler said. "I've detailed Kaporal Alfons Goetz to assist you in any way you think practical. He's out on assignment just now, but you'll get to meet him soon enough."

"That will be most helpful," the detective said, appre-ciatively. "I can probably put him to good use."

"I'll arrange for our next meeting to take place out-side of this office, for security reasons," the lieutenant then said. "We've had one or two embarrassing leaks from this department in recent months."

"Tip-offs?" Mason asked, in surprise.

"Call me from your hotel when you are ready," the other explained, side-stepping his query, "and I'll give you directions to St Wilfrid's. In the meantime, take care."

chapter 2

GEORGE MASON JOINED enthusiastically in the recessional hymn, *To be a Pilgrim*, at the conclusion of the 10.00 a.m. service the following Sunday, it being one of his favorites. He had located St. Wilfrid's well ahead of time in a narrow, tree-fringed street off a large open square called Pfauen, the site of the Kunsthaus, the city's main art gallery, pausing only to admire the famous bronze sculpture by Auguste Rodin set against the outer wall.

The vicar gave him a curt nod on his way to the vestry to disrobe, accompanied by two young female altar servers. Some members of the congregation hovered about the narthex to socialize, while others left promptly to attend to their affairs. The detective interested himself briefly in the selection of books and pamphlets on display, before he was approached by a slim, dark-haired young woman, apparently in charge of the bookstall.

"Looking for something in particular?" she asked, genially. "We have quite a wide selection."

Mason could have mentioned a few interesting titles he was looking for. Instead he simply said:

"Just browsing."

She moved away momentarily, to get a cup of coffee just now being served from a small table set farther back. When she returned, she said:

"Help yourself to refreshments, if you wish. There's no charge."

Mason acted on the suggestion, took coffee and a digestive biscuit and hovered in the vicinity of the bookstall, while the young woman completed the sale of a C.S. Lewis title. As he enjoyed his light refreshment, a second young woman, noticing that he was alone, came to his rescue. Her opening gambit told him at once that she was an American.

"Hi," she said, expansively. "Jill Crabtree."

"George Mason," the detective replied.

"Just passing through?" she enquired, marking him for a tourist.

"Not exactly," he replied, much taken by her open manner. "A business assignment, in a manner of speaking. And you?"

"Oh, I live in Zurich," she explained. "Moved here three years ago."

"From?"

"Boston, Massachusetts."

"Quite a change for you, I expect."

"I love it here, but it is of course very different. A much slower pace of life."

"And you have employment here?" he asked.

"I'm the registrar at the International School," she explained, "just across the lake."

At this point, the bookstall assistant joined them.

"Let me introduce myself," she offered. "Margaret Fern. I work for Succor, a human rights organization, something on the lines of Amnesty International."

"Indeed," said Mason, impressed. "Very commendable *and* challenging, I expect."

"Actually," the young woman explained, rather diffidently, "I just do the routine administrative tasks, supporting the legal team on their varied caseloads. Almost anything can crop up these days."

"I bet!" he replied.

"Mr Mason is here on business," Jill Crabtree put in.

"Did you enjoy the service?" Margaret Fern enquired, abruptly changing the subject, as if talk of work was best left to weekdays.

"In so far as I could follow it, not being too familiar with these modern rites. I did greatly enjoy the music, however. A first-rate organist you've got."

"Yes," Margaret agreed.. "Dr Hurlimann is a retired professor of music. We're very fortunate to have secured his services. And he trains the choir, very ably. Always looking for new recruits." She gave him a rather pointed look, but he averted his eyes. It was a long time since he had done any singing.

"If you're going to be in Zurich for a while," the American said, in her outgoing manner, "why not join us this evening, to find out more of what we do? A group of us meet regularly Sunday evenings for cheese fondue at the Wienerwald. At 7 p.m., if you can make it?"

"Will do my best," the detective agreed, inwardly gratified at the invitation and pleased that he had been so readily accepted into the church community.

"Now, if you'll excuse us," Margaret said, as most of the stay-behind members had departed, "we should now start clearing up a bit, to help the vicar's wife, Marjorie."

"Until later, then," Mason said, returning his cup before stepping outside into the bright late-morning sunshine.

It was shortly before midday by the time he reached the Hauptbahnhof on foot, to purchase *The Sunday Times* from the station kiosk. He tucked the bulky newspaper under one arm and strolled back along the river embankment, pausing every now and then to appraise the window displays of the boutiques selling local crafts, antiques and artworks. Medieval Russian icons vied with modern paintings by Braque and Matisse, all with price-tags well beyond his means. But Zurich was a well-heeled city; there would be no lack of wealthy art patrons. It also had a distinct medieval aspect, where the buildings of the Altstadt—the old city—crowded down to the river's edge, leaving narrow covered walkways to negotiate, at a fair remove from motor traffic and the trams that plied smoothly along the opposite bank, known as the Limmatquai.

Having reached the point where the river emerged from the lake, he crossed the final bridge and found himself at a busy junction called Belle Vue, fronted on one side by the Opera House, at right angles to a large restaurant called Gruene Heinrich, at whose pavement tables Zurchers were already seated for an early lunch. A wide promenade followed the shore of the lake into the distance and, since it was going to be a fine afternoon, he aimed to explore it in the hope of finding a lakeside café where he could enjoy a leisurely lunch and pass the afternoon catching up on news from England. Noting the well-appointed Wienerwald restaurant on his left, a few hundred yards from Belle Vue, he continued his stroll, watching the yachts tack into the stiff breeze coming down from the mountains to the south, clearly visible with their snow-capped peaks. As he walked, the stately buildings on the embankment gave way to large lawned areas, where young people he took to be students gathered in small groups for picnics or played desultory ball or hoop games. Some of the girls were doing callisthenics.

Continuing to the broadest part of the lake, he eventually came across exactly the sort of establishment he was seeking, a garden restaurant, with tables and umbrella shades right at the water's edge. He chose a table in the shade of a large beech-tree, but it was many minutes before the lone waiter approached him and that suited George Mason. Patrons were rather sparse so early in the season, so there would be no pressure to complete his meal and vacate his place. After a while, he scanned the brief menu, ordered lake trout with boiled potatoes and a stein of the local brew, opened his newspaper and prepared for an agreeable few hours by the Zurichsee, musing from time to time on what awaited him later that day at the Wienerwald, in addition to the pleasant company of Jill and Margaret. As for cheese fondue, what on earth was that?

<hr />

"Don't say you've never tried it before," Margaret Fern remarked, when George Mason found himself seated that evening in the spacious indoor dining-room of the Wienerwald, already half-full of diners.

"I'll give it a go," he replied, feeling there was a first time for everything. "But what exactly is cheese fondue?" He was much more familiar with English cheeses, the likes of Cheddar and Wensleydale.

"A mixture of Emmenthaler and Gruyere," Margaret explained. "From different parts of Switzerland."

"They're heated in white wine and kirsch, a liqueur of black cherries," Jill Crabtree put in, enthusiastically, "with lots of garlic and a dash of nutmeg. It's a Swiss speciality and really delicious."

"Sounds it," the detective replied, feeling his appetite stirring again following his long afternoon walk.

At that point, two youngish-looking men approached their table, increasing the complement to five.

"Sorry we're a bit late," the taller man explained. "Dr Hurlimann phoned as we were leaving. Wanted to sort out the hymns for next Sunday."

George Mason rose to his feet, as the two newcomers appraised him carefully.

"By the way," Margaret said, effecting the introductions. "This is George Mason."

"Max Fifield," the taller man said, offering his hand.

"Hugh Selby," the shorter man said, more genially.

"Very pleased to meet you," Mason said warmly, as both men took their seats.

"I was just about to order," Margaret said, as one of the several waiters hovered conveniently near their table.

"Better order a full carafe of fondant wine," Max said, with an air of authority marking him as obvious leader of the group, "if there are five of us. So, Mr Mason, what brings you to Zurich?"

"He was at the morning service," Margaret explained, "and Jill thoughtfully invited him out, to meet people."

The smart waiter arrived just then and took their order of fondue for five with accompanying white wine.

"I'm in the travel business," Mason explained, as instructed. "Researching itineraries for group tours by motor coach."

"Any particular theme?" Max wanted to know, warming to the idea.

"Cultural events and gastronomy," Mason replied.

"That's a great concept," Max observed. "And there should be plenty of scope hereabouts."

"I'm not so sure," Hugh Selby put in. "Cultural events, yes. But for food, I should think you'd be better off doing

France. Did a gastronomic tour of the Dordogne myself last year. Out of this world."

"You can get French and Italian cuisine, as well as German, in various parts of Switzerland," Margaret countered. "*And* there's the magnificent scenery."

"Quite right," Max said, authoritatively. "I may be able to give you a few pointers myself, in fact. I travel around quite a lot."

"Max is a sales representative for a well-known book publisher," Jill explained.

Mention of books piqued Mason's immediate interest. He glanced at Max Fifield for elaboration. Max took the cue.

"Manfred Bott AG, of Bern," he offered. "Academic publishers, supplying textbooks and related materials to universities and colleges."

"And your territory?" Mason enquired.

"Oh, anywhere north or south of the Alps, including southern Germany and northern Italy. My colleagues cover central Switzerland."

Konstanz and Luino, two locations of missing books, came at once to the detective's mind. Both places, curiously enough, would be in Fifield's territory. But his musings were interrupted by the arrival of the fondue, served with some ceremony. The waiter placed the large bowl of pungent cheese over a low flame in the middle of the table and then served a platter piled high with cubes of white bread. The diners leaned forward in keen anticipation, inhaling the heady vapors of the dish.

"What happens now?" asked a bemused Mason.

"It's quite straightforward," Jill said, helpfully. "Just take a cube of bread, skewer it firmly with your fork and dip it into the cheese until well-coated. Then you eat it."

"Watch you don't burn your mouth," Hugh Selby cautioned. "It may be quite hot, especially at first."

The detective waited for the others to begin, before making his own dip, thinking what a sociable meal it was, with everyone eating from the same bowl. A couple of mouthfuls soon convinced him that this was indeed something he would greatly enjoy, the dry white wine providing the perfect foil. The atmosphere of the Wienerwald was further enhanced by the arrival of a pianist, who began playing popular classics on a grand piano over in the far corner of the room.

"Sounds like a Debussy arabesque," the knowledgeable Margaret Fern said.

"Well done, Meg," Max Fifield remarked, using her pet name. "I would never have guessed."

They all listened appreciatively until the piece was concluded, while making frequent dips into the diminishing bowl of melted cheese. Max Fifield adjusted the flame lower so that, as he explained to the newcomer, the cheese wouldn't cake too hard on the bottom.

"Tell me more about Succor, Margaret," Mason said. "What they actually do."

"You may call me Meg, if you like," she replied. "Everyone else does. The top priority with us right now is the plight of young girls, mainly from East Europe and some from North Africa, who are lured to western European countries by bogus offers of employment as store assistants, waitresses and the like."

"You mean these job offers don't materialize?" a none-too-surprised George Mason enquired.

"Unfortunately not," Meg explained. "Their passports are confiscated and they are sold on to pimps, who use them unscrupulously to pay off the purchase price. In plain language, it's a form of slavery."

"Incredible," said Mason, deeply concerned, "that a woman can be bought and sold like a chattel, in this day and age."

"All manner of things go on in this day and age," Jill Crabtree said, pensively, "that law enforcement can't seem to do much about."

The detective nodded in complete agreement at that remark, thinking it just as well they were not aware of his true profession. Police work was often a question of time, resources, manpower and priorities, not necessarily in that order.

"Some of the victims manage to escape, often at great risk to themselves," Meg then added. "That's where we come in. We shelter them, give them counseling and help them return to their former homes."

"Meg is very dedicated," Jill remarked. "She often puts up escapees in her own apartment, when the hostel in Rapperswil is full."

"Very commendable," the detective said, glancing in genuine admiration at this modest-seeming young woman, who had now begun chipping at the crusted base of the fondue dish, perhaps to distract attention from herself.

"This bit tastes best of all," she said, offering Mason some to try, while the others also fished in prospectively.

"M-mm," uttered Mason, savoring it. "I see what you mean." It had the texture of toasted cheese, with a concentrated after-taste of kirsch.

The book salesman noted with satisfaction the look of contentment on the newcomer's face.

"Did it meet your expectations?" he enquired, genially.

"Absolutely," Mason replied, with conviction. "It's a real get-together meal. I'll certainly recommend it to my tour clients."

"We don't normally take dessert," Jill said, matter-of-factly. "Just coffee. But if you're still hungry, I can recommend the apple strudel."

Mason, conscious of his waistline, brushed aside the suggestion.

"I'll plump for coffee, too," he said, as they settled back into their chairs and enjoyed the piano playing, while the waiter cleared the table and took their order for coffee. After a few moments' relaxation, the detective turned his attention to the second young man, who was drumming the piano tune on the tablecloth with his finger tips.

"I expect you have an interesting job here, too," he observed.

"I'm a translator," Hugh Selby came back at once, leaning forward in his chair, so that Mason could hear his rather small voice over the background noise.

"Freelance?"

"Actually, no," Hugh explained. "I work for the Federal Immigration Bureau, dealing mainly with applications for asylum."

"I expect you have to know quite a few languages for that," Mason proposed.

"French and Spanish are the main ones."

"I imagine it involves some travel, too?" Mason was fishing, trying to establish if Selby moved about the country, like Max Fifield.

"Mainly desk work," Hugh said, a touch ruefully. "Apart from the odd trip to Bern for conferences. That's a nice route for you, George, through the Bernese Oberland by rail."

"Rail travel is very popular in Switzerland, I believe," Mason said.

"Because the railways are so efficient," Max put in. "I always use them myself. Wouldn't dream of going by car."

A useful admission possibly, the detective reflected, as coffee was served with a dark chocolate for each cup, and the gifted pianist launched into a medley of Chopin waltzes. The Wienerwald by now was completely full, with prospective patrons forming a small queue in the foyer. The clock had moved on to 9 pm.

"Where would I best get information on events in Zurich?" Mason enquired, of no one in particular, taking advantage of a brief lull in the conversation.

"From *Tages Anzeiger*," Jill came back at once. "It's a daily newspaper that carries lots of advertisements and announcements. They'll most likely have it at your hotel."

"I'll make a point of asking for it at breakfast," Mason said.

"Now, if you'll all excuse me," Jill said, rising to leave and placing her contribution to the meal on the table, "school starts early in Switzerland. See you at choir practice on Wednesday."

"May I make a small request, before you go?" Mason asked.

"By all means," they all chimed, in chorus.

"I'd very much appreciate a group photograph, as a souvenir of this happy occasion," he explained, fumbling in his jacket pocket for his camera.

Jill Crabtree, with a look of amused surprise, resumed her seat momentarily. The group then quickly arranged themselves for a snapshot, evidently happy enough to oblige the unpredictable newcomer. The little ritual completed, Mason replaced the camera in his pocket, as Jill Crabtree got up to leave.

"How about a small liqueur with the coffee," Max Fifield proposed. "just to round off a successful evening? Then I too shall have to leave. Early start tomorrow, I'm afraid."

"Make mine a straight cognac," the detective said with satisfaction, feeling well-pleased with the evening's events.

"I'll have a Drambuie," Hugh Selby said. "What about you, Meg?"

"I think I'll pass, this time." she unexpectedly replied. "More coffee would be fine."

chapter 3

GEORGE MASON ROSE early the following morning and went down to the hotel dining-room to order a typical Swiss breakfast of Birchermuesli—a bowl of mixed cereals, nuts and yoghourt topped with fresh fruit. A healthy way to start the day, he reflected, relishing the memory of his gourmet meal the previous evening. When he had finished eating, he went over to the newspaper rack, found the current edition of *Tages Anzeiger* and flicked through it while finishing his coffee. Max Fifield was correct. The journal published notices of the day's main events in both the city and canton of Zurich. One item in particular caught his eye; it was a book fair to be held that very afternoon at Rutli Meadow on the shores of Lake Lucerne. On the assumption that stolen books had to resurface somewhere, for their value to be realized, such fairs might be as good a place as any to try and trace them, especially since the newspaper notice made specific reference to antiquarian items. On his way out, he rang Harrington from the hotel foyer and asked him to do routine checks on the backgrounds of Max Fifield, Hugh Selby and Margaret Fern, on the off-chance that something useful might turn up.

It was a bright, sunny day, with a fresh breeze coming off the lake, as he made his way unhurriedly along the Limmatquai, to cover the half-mile or so distance to the main station, dropping off at a pharmacy on the way to have his snap of the fondue party developed, along with several views he had taken of the city during his first few days there. When he reached the Hauptbahnhof, he discovered that trains to Lucerne left every hour, on the hour, leaving him a wait of twenty minutes before making the 10 a.m. express the locals called the *Schnellzug*. He passed the interval, after purchasing a return ticket, browsing at the magazine stands on the large, modern concourse leading to upwards of twenty platforms, for services to different parts of the continent, to cities such as Vienna, Milan and Barcelona. It was a major hub of railway traffic, Mason concluded, surveying the exotic destinations on the indicator board, as he boarded his own train with a few minutes to spare.

About an hour later, he emerged from Lucerne Station to be greeted by an elegant medium-sized city fronting a vast expanse of lake. There were scores of tourists about, strolling with their cameras along the broad promenades or veering inland towards the craft stalls and art galleries on the embankment, near where a long covered bridge, built entirely of wood, led across a swift-flowing river to an area of small hotels and riverside restaurants just now preparing for the lunch-hour trade. He enquired of a policeman how to reach Rutli Meadow and was directed to a large paddle-steamer, the *S.S. Uri*.

As he waited his turn to board, behind a large group of Japanese, he marveled at the size and construction of the vessel looming before him, with its huge paddle-wheel rising high above the waterline, berthed less than a hundred yards from the station exit. Launched in the late nineteenth-century, it was over a hundred years old and amazingly still doing sterling service on the lake, which stretched as far as the eye could see, towards the distant alps. It left promptly at 11.30, Mason positioning himself on the lower deck near one of the paddle-wheels, so that he could watch through the observation window as it slowly began to rotate and move the vintage vessel away from the quay, driven by powerful pistons in the engine room.

Having satisfied his curiosity about the mechanics, he ascended to the main deck and made a brief tour of the *Uri*. It was much like an ocean liner, if on a smaller scale, with lounges, a library, a choice of restaurants, deckchairs in the open areas. The second-class amenity, forward of the main deck, had already filled with groups of schoolchildren and their minders buying snacks and drinks. Small chance of refreshment there, for the duration of the voyage, Mason reflected, making his way to the upper deck and the far more commodious first-class dining-room, its tables covered with crisp linen cloths. As there were no vacant tables even here, he found a window seat opposite an elderly gentleman engrossed in a book. He sat down and observed with interest the passing scenery, the large islands on whose near-vertical rock faces hardy pines managed, incredibly, to cling. Small, picturesque villages dotted the tree-lined shore. After a while, he glanced at the luncheon menu, summoned the waiter and placed his order.

At that juncture, his table companion laid aside his reading and glanced at him.

"From England?" he tentaively enquired

"How did you guess?" Mason asked, a little piqued that it was so obvious.

"Your accent," the other replied, "when ordering lunch. On vacation in Switzerland?"

"In a manner of speaking."

"Then you have come to the right place. Lucerne is one of the most beautiful parts of the country…and very historic."

"You are referring to Rutli Meadow?" Mason enquired.

"Where the *S.S. Uri* is now headed. We should reach it in about two hours."

"I read about it briefly in my guidebook," Mason said.

"It is no less than the place where the Swiss nation was born," the other said, enthusiastically. "By the way, I am a retired schoolmaster from Zug. Franz Hassler."

"George Mason," the detective said. "Glad to make your acquaintance."

"*Gleichfalls*," Franz replied, reverting unconsciously to his native tongue.

"Weren't there just three original cantons involved?"

"Exactly so," Franz said, evidently pleased that the visitor knew something at least. "The cantons of Schwyz, Uri and Unterwalden made a defensive pact in 1291 against the Austrians, their oppressive overlords."

"Is that where William Tell comes on the scene?"

"He was what today would be called a freedom fighter. He escaped from the enemy in a fierce storm at the top of the lake and managed to kill the harsh Austrian governor with a bolt from his crossbow."

"Is there some record of that?" the curious visitor wanted to know.

"The Chapel of William Tell, built to commemorate his daring escapade," Franz explained, "was erected at the very spot where he entered the lake. But that's much farther on, where the mountains rise up sheer from the water, towering above it. The *Uri* doesn't go quite so far on this trip. Try it's sister ship, the *Fluellen*."

George Mason, quite fascinated, took it all in as the waiter served his lake trout with French fries and a light beer; while the former teacher placed a modest order for a grilled ham-and-cheese sandwich, with a bottle of mineral water. All this local knowledge would, he realized, help strengthen his credentials as a tour scout when tackled on the subject at St Wilfrid's.

"Other cantons joined them in the course of time," Franz went on, "to create the modern nation we proudly have today."

"One that has maintained its independence," Mason observed, admiringly, "through all the wars and upheavals of the last several centuries."

"Correct again," Franz said, warming to his appreciative new acquaintance, while watching him tackle with gusto his tasty meal. "We celebrate our nationhood at the site every year on August 1st. And there's something else you may not know. After the German invasion of Austria in World War 11, the Swiss army officers met at Rutli Meadow to pledge resistance to enemy incursions down to the last fighting man."

"Amazing," said the detective, genuinely impressed.

"We are a citizens' army." Franz proudly explained. "Every male within certain age-limits undergoes military training for several weeks each year. It's obligatory."

"You yourself," asked Mason, "did you bear arms while teaching in Zug?"

"During the summer recess," Franz replied. "I only began my career at Zug. Later on, I moved to Zurich, after obtaining a post at the International School. I retired only last year, in fact."

"Indeed?" Mason said. "I know someone who works there, as registrar."

"Jill Crabtree," Franz came back at once. "A lovely person, *and* a very accomplished soprano."

"She sings in the choir at St Wilfrid's Community Church."

Franz Hassler smiled knowingly and nodded.

"I used to attend the carol concerts they give every Christmas. A notable event in the city's music calendar, I may say. Jill often sang a solo item. How is she these days?"

"Seemed just fine to me," the detective replied, "as of yesterday evening at the Wienerwald restaurant, over a cheese fondue."

Hassler's panini sandwich then arrived, occupying his full attention, as George Mason nudged his empty plate aside and nursed his beer, glancing through the dining-room window to marvel at the ever-changing vistas.

"A wonderful person, Jill, in so many ways," the former teacher suddenly remarked. "And yet..."

Mason looked at him questioning surprise.

"Perhaps I shouldn't mention this," Franz continued, half-apologetically, "but there was some kind of question mark against her name a while ago."

"A question mark?" the astonished detective countered, wondering what on earth could be the nature of the forthcoming revelations.

"Nothing was proven against her, of course," Franz hurried to explain. "Before taking up her post as registrar at the International School, which also involves responsibility for the school budget, she held a similar position at a private school in Freiburg."

"Freiburg?" Mason asked, uncertainly.

"A major city in the French-speaking region, over by the Jura Mountains to the west," the academic said. "I got it from my brother-in-law, who taught at the same school for a while, that certain irregularities where found in the school accounts during Jill's tenure."

"But surely," Mason protested, "she would not have obtained her present post if she had had problems at Freiburg?"

"No charges were leveled against her, I do know that," Franz maintained. "And the whole business blew over, according to my brother-in-law, in a matter of weeks."

"To avoid a scandal," Mason suggested.

"Perhaps," agreed the Swiss. "Or perhaps, on the other hand, she was not too competent at book-keeping. American systems are rather different from our own. When external auditors were brought in, the problems were eventually resolved."

George Mason sat back and drank more beer, feeling a curious sense of relief, even though as yet he hardly knew the woman. Was such a disclosure relevant to his professional enquiries, or was it not? That was the significant question. Incompetence was one thing, embezzlement quite another.

"You will, of course," Franz beseeched, "hold my remarks in complete confidence?"

The detective noticed a sudden slowing of the boat's engines, indicating that they were approaching the dock

"Absolutely," he replied. "You can count on me. This your stop?"

"Er..no," Franz said. "I'm continuing on to Fluellen to visit my niece, then catching the *Schnellzug* direct to Zurich later this evening." He rose from his chair to shake Mason's hand warmly as the detective, now that the engines were silent, made to leave the dining-room and join the disembarkation queue at the gangway.

Several minutes later, he found himself back on terra firma in the historic environs of Rutli Meadow, pausing only to watch the large paddle-wheels of the *S.S. Uri* start to rotate again as it moved slowly away from the quay. His eye followed its stately progess for a while, marveling at its graceful lines as it soon picked up speed and headed south towards the mountains, before turning his attention to the large stretch of meadow opening before him, bordered on one side by the lake, on the other by dense woodland. A white marquee dominated the scene, with refreshment stalls near the entrance and, to Mason's pleasant surprise, a Swiss in leather knickerbockers blowing sonorously on a fifteen-foot alpine horn, the sort of thing he imagined they used to call in cattle off the high pastures.

The book fair had attracted quite a good crowd, he discovered, as he made his way in. The material was laid out on separate tables, which were stocked by subject. Unsure if Ernest Hemingway came under Classical Fiction or Modern Fiction, he opted for the former and found himself confronted by volumes of Goethe, Trollope, Balzac and Dickens. Evidently, the author of *The Old Man and the Sea* was classed as a modern and, sure enough, on the adjoining table he found some fine first editions, a couple of them signed, of *For Whom the Bell Tolls* and *The Sun Also Rises*. Handling them gingerly, to admire the dust-jackets, he was also intrigued at the prices they were expected to fetch, shown in pencil on the fly-leaf. 2500 francs for a regular copy; 15,000 francs for a signed one. An appreciable difference, he considered; but no doubt worth it to a serious collector. He could appreciate why people wanted to own these beautiful objects, even though collecting had never personally appealed to him. The stall assistant, an attractive young woman clad in dirndl bodice and skirt, eyed him expectantly; but he was in no mind to buy at such keen prices, and he could hardly tell her he was trying to trace stolen property.

The stall marked Architecture was his next stop, stocked with large, heavy tomes lying flat on the table. Skewing his head sideways to read the spines, he soon discerned a well-preserved copy of Palladio's *Architettura* in its handsome binding. He opened it carefully, feeling his pulse quicken, under the watchful eye of a professorial-looking gentleman. A cursory examination soon informed him, however, that this was a *secondo edizione*, but still worth 20,000 francs. He leafed through it for a few moments, admiring the colored plates, before moving on round the table, where he found a French translation of the same item dating from the nineteenth century, at a much lower price. At least, he reflected, proceeding to the History table, he now had a much clearer idea of the stolen property, which alone justified his day-trip. Chief Inspector Harrington was sure to be impressed.

No editions of Ackerman's *History of Westminster Abbey* were to be found on the History stall, as he browsed among the piled tomes of mainly Victorian provenance, bearing titles such as Gibbons' *Decline and Fall of the Roman Empire,* Tocqueville's *America* and Carlyle's *The French Revolution.* These were relatively few in number, compared to the numerous volumes in German and French, predominantly by Swiss authors unfamiliar to him. Trade was fairly brisk here and he soon found himself feeling redundant, allowing himself a quick glance at the Art section, especially at prints of Van Gogh that invariably intrigued him for their astonishing use of color. Quitting the marquee to further explore Rutli Meadow in the cool sunshine, he left time for another beer and a Dutch cigar on the terrace of the lakeside *Stube*, from where he could observe the yachts tacking fitfully across the lake and the bustle on the quay. The *S.S.*

Uri was due to call in another forty-five minutes, on its return trip from Fluellen.

.

⌖

Two days later, he presented himself for choir practice. Following Herr Hassler's confidential disclosure about Jill Crabtree, for what it was worth, he thought it advisable to keep in as close contact as possible with people at St Wilfrid's. They were pleasantly surprised to see him, particularly since he could add some weight to the bass section, most of the male singers, including Hugh Selby, being tenors. Max Fifield handed him copies of the music and guided him through a rehearsal of a Vaughan Williams anthem they were preparing for Whit Sunday. The intrepid detective did his best in the circumstances, and if he botched a few notes there was nobody about to complain about it. There would be time enough for improvements. Max Fifield was in fact quite complimentary afterwards; while the organist-cum-choir master thanked him warmly for his contribution.

It was late-evening when they emerged from the building, the quartet from the Wienerwald breaking away from the rest of the choir after taking their leave of Dr Hurlimann. Mason fell in step with them automatically, until they reached the doorway of a small *Stube* called The Waldman, a short distance from the church.

"Won't you join us for a nightcap, George?" Margaret Fern enquired, as the group was about to enter.

"Yes, please do," Jill Crabtree urged, noting his slight hesitation.

"Don't mind if I do," the detective replied. "It's thirsty work, all that singing, especially if you're not so used to it."

"You'll soon get used to it," Max promised, leading the way inside.

Stooping beneath the low lintel, they gained the cramped interior of the inn. The waitress showed them to a corner table and immediately took their order, the men wanting beers and the two women coffee. Mason's eye took in the details of the room. It was warmly decorated in traditional Swiss style, with deep-red drapes at the doors and windows and alpine motifs, such as cowbells and edelweiss, on the walls. It was about half full with patrons enjoying a late dinner. Pasta dishes, mainly, in so far as he could observe, making a mental note to try it some time for his evening meal.

"You managed that fairly well, George," Max remarked, as soon as they were comfortably seated and the women had returned from the restroom. "You've obviously done part-singing before."

"Quite a while ago," Mason confessed. "At my local church."

"In Clitheroe, would that be?" Max wanted to know.

The detective nodded, maintaining his subterfuge. In any case, it was close enough to the truth.

"It takes us ages to learn a new piece," Margaret said. "Don't be discouraged if you find it hard at first. We're all just amateurs."

Mason noted the slight frown that crossed Max's features at that remark, as if he considered himself rather more than an amateur. But he held his peace.

"So what have you discovered these last few days, George, on behalf of Bowland Tours?" Hugh Selby wanted to know, as their drinks arrived with a complimentary bowl of pretzels.

Jill and Margaret, feeling peckish, dipped at once into the welcome snack and sipped their coffees attentively.

"Did you manage to get a copy of *Tages Anzeiger*, as I suggested?" Max enquired.

George Mason answered both questions as one.

"I certainly did," he replied, with a nod towards Max. "And on Monday I read a notice in it about an antiquarian book fair at Rutli Meadow."

As he spoke, he watched his table companions closely, for any involuntary reaction to the mention of rare books. But he discerned none; in fact, they all seemed very much intrigued.

"So you went right over there, did you?" Hugh asked. "On the ferry from Lucerne?"

Mason nodded and quaffed his beer.

"It would make a great trip for English tourists," he said, eventually. "I didn't spend much time in Lucerne itself, but that should be worth at least half a day. Then there's the two-hour sail by paddle-steamer that takes you most of the way up Lake Lucerne to Rutli Meadow and its intriguing historical associations. I had a great day out."

The quartet smilingly approved of his adventure, evidently pleased with his discovery.

"You're one up on me," Margaret said. "I've never been there."

"You don't know Swiss history," Hugh put in. "That's where the Swiss Confederation all began. William Tell and all that."

"Find any interesting books?" Max abruptly asked, almost catching the detective off his guard.

"Wasn't really in the market," Mason replied. "Just browsing, that's all."

"But you must have some interest in old books," Max persisted, "to choose that particular venue."

Mason drank some more beer, thinking quickly to avoid a possible trap.

"A passing interest," he replied. "Mainly in vintage travel books, the ones with photographic plates."

"And did you have any success?" Jill enquired, much intrigued, as Max Fifield seemed fully to accept his improvisation.

"Not really," Mason said, with mock disappointment. "A good selection of novels, I thought. And histories, philosophy, most of them in the old Gothic German script. Outside the marquee, there was even a demonstration of the alpine horn." He aimed to switch their attention away from books.

"That's interesting," Hugh remarked. "You should also try to locate a demonstration of cowbell ringing. They have them from time to time, mainly in country districts."

"Cowbell ringing?" asked an incredulous Mason.

"They play them as hand bells," Hugh explained. "A small group of performers, each with a different-sized bell, ringing in harmony. A virtual symphony, you might say. I heard them in Appenzell last year."

"Quite amazing," the detective said, pleased that they had changed the subject. "Alpine horns, cowbells. Whatever next?"

"Yodeling," Margaret came back at once. "You simply must try to attend a yodeling competition. Look out for notices in *Tages Anzeiger.*"

"I'll do that," Mason said, gratefully accepting the tip.

The cuckoo clock on the wall suddenly sprang to life, the bird popping out ten times to mark the hour.

"Gosh," exclaimed Jill. "Is it that time already?"

It was the cue to summon the waitress and settle their accounts, as they drained their drinks and prepared to leave.

"Before I forget," Jill then said. "I may not make it back in time for the Kantorei rehearsal on Friday."

"Why ever not?" a solicitous Hugh Selby enquired.

"It's Founder's Day at school," she explained. "After the special assembly in the morning—the guest speaker, by the way, is none other than our vicar—we have the rest of the day off. So I'm taking the opportunity to visit a friend in Bellinzona. The earliest train I can catch is the 12.10, so I don't expect to be back before 9 p.m., at the earliest."

"The Kantorei is a concert choir," Margaret Fern explained, noting Mason's interest. "We're rehearsing a Mozart Mass to perform at the Tonhalle in August. But I don't suppose you'll be here by then; otherwise we could have got you a complimentary ticket."

"We shall have to see how things develop," the detective said, non-commitally, as the group got up to leave. Once outside The Waldman, he observed with interest that Max Fifield and Jill Crabtree walked off together in one direction, while Margaret Fern and Hugh Selby took another. He also made a mental note to inform Leutnant Kubler of the American's travel plans.

chapter 4

Count Flavio di Montesedina awoke early on Friday morning and, as it promised to be a sunny day, took his espresso on the patio of his small villa at Stresa overlooking Lake Maggiore and the southern tip of Isola Bella, a large island a mile off-shore. The size of his dwelling was an indication of his reduced circumstances. Of a proud aristocratic family which traced its lineage as far back as the Quattrocento, when one of the Renaissance popes had granted his ancestor estates in Umbria, he was hard put to maintain the minimum acceptable standard of living for someone of his position. Three years ago, he had downsized from his ancestral seat in the Appenines, dismissed his retainers save for an aged cook-housekeeper, and taken up permanent residence in the Villa Serena. Periodically, he drove his aging Alfa Romeo to inspect his vineyards near Foligno, which he had placed in the capable hands of a paid manager and vintner, who oversaw every stage in the production of *Casa Montesedina*, an upmarket red, and *Fiore di Foligno*, a peachy white rather similar to Soave.

His housekeeper, Signora Giacinta, served him his customary light breakfast or *collazione* at the patio table, bearing a tray of fresh rolls, damson jam, a modest portion of prosciutto ham and fruit juice. In his early sixties, he was a man of modest appetite in accordance with his means, who kept himself in fairly good trim taking long morning walks along the lakeshore. He generally rose before his wife Amelia, ten years his junior, a watercolorist who rented a small studio a short distance from the villa.

"Is the Signora Amelia awake yet?" he enquired of Giacinta.

"Just now stirring," the aged housekeepr said, amiably. "She will be down later, but will take only coffee and grape juice for breakfast. You are to begin without her."

"Is she going to her studio today?' he then asked.

"I believe so."

"Good," replied the count. "Since I shall be away most of the day. Please tell her, if she's not down before I leave, that I have business in Bellinzona. Shan't be back for dinner."

Giacinta's face brightened at the mention of that historic town in Ticino, the southern and Italian-speaking part of Switzerland. It was her birthplace, which she had left on her marriage to a Piedmontese journeyman named Renzo.

"Will signor be taking the car?" she enquired.

"Actually no," the count replied. "I prefer the train. It's just too long a drive."

With that, he enjoyed his modest repast in solitude, as the sun rose higher over the lake, reflecting brightly in its clear waters; as the birdsong in the cypresses and willows surrounding the villa rose to a crescendo. Sparrows hopped onto his breakfast table, snapping up the crumbs he casually left for them. He went quickly up to his room to dress in good time to cover the fifteen-minute walk to Stresa Station, where he would board the morning express from Milan to Locarno.

Once seated in his crowded compartment and glancing at the passing scenery, reflecting ruefully that in former days he would have traveled first-class, he mulled over the reasons for his less affluent circumstances. As he saw it, the downturn began not very long after Italy entered the Common Market. The freer competition meant that he had to cut his margins and trim the prices of his wines to retain market share. The unusually wet summer two years ago had depleted his harvest to the point almost of bankruptcy. And now there was this new threat from the European Union to cut subsidies to viticulture and reduce the size of the wine lake, that reservoir of overproduced, lower-quality vintages held off the market to maintain prices. There was even talk of using wines for industrial purposes. He shuddered to think what those might be. Industrial wine! The very notion was a travesty. The future held many uncertainties, but one thing was assured: the bureaucrats in Brussels would oblige estates like his to uproot at least a third of their vines, further cutting his income.

As a Count of Montesedina, with its ancient lineage, he had long been of a mind to do something about what he considered unwarranted and disastrous intervention into centuries-old ways of life. Why, even the shepherds were fast disappearing from his native countryside, to satisfy the conservationist lobby and make room for wild boars, wolves, bears and other so-called threatened species; for national parks, golf courses, ski areas and sundry recreational amenities. The Italy he had grown up in would soon be unrecognizable if firm action wasn't taken, and taken soon. Nor was he the only grower to ponder along these lines. He met regularly with colleagues in the farming community, to share these concerns. The key question was, would they be able to reverse the likely course of events?

The express stopped briefly at Verbania before continuing on to Cannero-Riviera, an attractive lakeside resort, where he alighted and commenced the steep walk downhill past the open-air market in the main square, to reach the lakeside jetty. While waiting a few minutes for the jetfoil ferry to return from the opposite shore, his gaze took in the magnificent vista of the southern alps rising massively at the northern tip of the lake, just across the border with Switzerland. Within half an hour he had crossed the water, making his way at a steady gait to cover the half-mile to Luino Station. There he caught the local train that wound through the villages nestled among the hills on the north-eastern side of Lake Maggiore, calling at each one. It was an hour's journey before this branch line, with its chugging locomotives, linked up with the main Swiss network at Bellinzona. Count Flavio was in no hurry. He sat back on the wooden bench-seat in an almost empty carriage and enjoyed the ever-changing view.

George Mason, seeking a change from his usual yoghourt and muesli, was finishing a breakfast of scrambled eggs and Walliserteller, an assortment of cold cuts of meat, while browsing through *Tages Anzeiger* for notices on the day's events, when he received a call from the hotel lobby to answer the phone. He eased his large frame out of his chair and repaired at once to the telephone booth by the reception desk, taking care to close the glass door firmly behind him.

"And how are the Swiss treating you?" came the faintly ironic voice of Chief Inspector Harrington.

"Can't complain, so far," Mason replied. "In fact, I'm rather enjoying things. Went to a fondue party recently and took a trip by paddle-steamer on Lake Lucerne."

"Lucky you," the senior man returned, with just a touch of envy. "But don't overstep your budget or I'll have the Commissioner breathing down my neck. Now listen carefully. We've checked out the backgrounds of those individuals you mentioned. They're all in the clear. No black marks against them, except speeding tickets for Hugh Selby. Seems he likes fast cars."

"Surprising," Mason remarked, thinking how staid and level-headed the young tenor appeared to be.

"But we did turn up something, whether useful or not, on Mr Max Fifield."

"Oh?" asked Mason, expectantly.

"Seems he was a local organiser for the Britannia Party, up until the last election, when they lost heavily."

"Isn't that the far-right outfit, anti-European, anti-immigration?"

"Just so," his chief replied. "The police keep tabs on them and their leadership in the event of riots, either instigated by them or directed at them. They have faced charges in the past for inciting minor disturbances, particularly at Milcaster and a few other hardscrabble northern towns, where unemployment tends to be above the average."

"Textile towns on the Pennines?"

"In the West Riding, mainly," Harrington replied. "Fifield was cautioned on one occasion, but not charged. Nothing against him since, presumably because he moved to Zurich in the meantime."

"He's in the book trade here," Mason said, carefully noting his superior's remarks, which he did not consider particularly significant. Many Britons had strong right-wing views.

"So he moves around quite a lot?" Harrington en-quired.

"Visiting universities and colleges, mainly in northern Switzerland and southern Germany as far as Stuttgart, from what I can gather."

"Worth keeping an eye on, then," Harrington said, "as a matter of routine."

"It's early days, yet," Mason replied. "But I have made a useful start. Managed to infiltrate the church community successfully. I even joined the choir!"

"Good for you, Inspector," his chief said, encourag-ingly. "Get that bass of yours out of mothballs. And let me know at once of any significant developments."

"I'll do that. In the meantime, contact the American Embassy in London and see if you can get any background on a Jill Crabtree, from Boston, Massachusetts."

"Will try my best," Harrington promised, ringing off.

While occupying the phone booth, the detective took the opportunity to ring his wife Adele, mainly to say hello, but also to check that she had made hotel reservations for the trip they were planning to the Lake District in Septem-ber, partly to mark their wedding anniversary. Having done that, he returned to the dining-room to finish his coffee, before setting off for the Polizei Dienst behind the Haupt-bahnhof. On his way along the Limmatquai, he stopped off at a pharmacy to get color prints of the group snapshot he had taken at the Wienerwald. He would then inform Leutnant Kubler of Jill Crabtree's itinerary that day. Herr Hassler's disclosures on the *S.S. Uri* a few days ago might not mean very much, but he was determined not to pass up even the slenderest of leads, in the hope of something use-ful turning up.

When Jill Crabtree passed through the barrier to Platform 8 just after noon, to board the Zurich-Milano express, she paid no attention to Kaporal Alfons Goetz, clad in a brown corduroy jacket, slacks and a Tyrolean hat, who was standing at the nearby bookstall holding a snapshot inside the pages of a copy of *Time* magazine. Nor was she aware that he had followed her onto the waiting train. She occupied a window seat she had pre-booked in a second-class non-smoking compartment and casually observed the last-minute bustle on the platform, before the train pulled promptly and smoothly out of the station on the two-hour trip to Bellinzona. As the tenements in a less-affluent part of her adopted city receded from view, she withdrew from her shoulder bag the copy of *The New York Times* she had purchased at the station kiosk, to catch up on the news from home. This was something of a special treat for her. Since the *Times* was only sold at the station kiosk, she rarely bought it unless shopping in town on Saturday morning or traveling somewhere by train.

Its thirty or so pages gave a wide coverage of national and international events and she was particularly intrigued to read the article on a threatened invasion of skinheads at Rutli Meadow, planned to disrupt the annual celebration of Swiss independence on August 1. Only rarely, in her experience, did the broadsheet cover events in Switzerland and it was a pity, she thought, that they had focused on something as negative as this. So absorbed was she in her reading that she paid little attention to the majestic scenery of the central alps whose snow-capped peaks rose massively above them; and they were already inside the interminable St Gotthard Tunnel before she laid the paper aside, unable to read as the lights dimmed. When the express duly emerged from the subterranean darkness, it would be only a short while before it reached Bellinzona.

She refolded the newspaper, placed it in her bag to finish reading on her return journey and focused her thoughts on the luncheon meeting that lay ahead, quite unaware that the Tyrolean-looking gentleman a few seats back and apparently reading *Time* magazine had her under close observation. Count Flavio was a childhood friend of her mother's. They grew up together in the Umbrian town of Foligno and had kept in fairly regular touch with each other since the day she had left Italy on her early marriage to an English wine merchant named Gordon Crabtree, whose firm had later sent him to the United States to open a branch in Boston, just as Americans were beginning to acquire a taste for imported table wines, among them the two main vintages from the Montesedina estate. Her mother was of minor Italian aristocracy, who shared many of the views held by Flavio de Montesedina, views she had over the years carefully inculcated in her daughter. So it was with a sense of anticipation, as the train emerged from the long tunnel to forge through the much gentler landscapes of Ticino, that Jill Crabtree approached her first ever meeting with the redoubtable count.

There were two men waiting to greet her as she stepped out onto the platform, the aging count and a much younger man introduced to her as Marco Villanuova. The count ushered them both into the spacious restaurant on the main concourse, where they occupied a corner table and briefly studied the menu.

"So happy to meet you at last," Flavio said. "Your mother has told me so much about you and about how well you are doing in Zurigo."

"It's a very pleasant city to live in," Jill replied, opting for a *salade nicoise*. "Rated in the top five cities in the world for quality of life."

The count smiled his enigmatic smile.

"Much too orderly for me," he observed. "I prefer the comparative chaos of Italy, the warmth of the landscape and the people. What say you, Marco?"

The younger man, in company with the count, ordered filet steak, pasta and a carafe of Italian red wine for the three of them.

"I've lived here in Ticino long enough to regard it as just an extension of northern Italy. The quality of life is much the same. North of the alps I cannot speak for, as I have never been to Zurich."

"Marco heads the music department at Collegio San Isidoro, a boarding school in the hills above Bellinzona," the count explained. "One of his responsibilities is the annual Pergolesi Festival, held in the grounds every summer."

"I'm not familiar with that composer at all," Jill said, half apologetically.

Luncheon arrived at that point and, as it was well past noon, they tackled it with keen appetites. Marco filled their wine glasses and proposed a toast 'to Italy'.

Eventually, he remarked: "Our aim at San Isidoro is to revive Pergolesi's music. At one period, he was immensely popular, particularly in Paris. But over the last hundred years or so, he has suffered a rather serious decline. We alternate our programs between one of his oratorios, such as *Stabat Mater*, and one of his operas, such as *The Maid as Mistress*."

"Seems a risky choice for a boys' boarding school," the conventionally-minded Flavio remarked. "Whatever do the parents make of it?"

"They join in the spirit of it," Marco laughed. "In fact, our boys perform both male and female roles. It can be quite hilarious, at times, believe me."

"And what do the Aurelian Brothers make of it? They're the religious order," he explained to the American, "who run San Isidoro."

"They much prefer the oratorios," the music master said, blandly.

"I just bet they do," returned the count, with emphasis.

As the luncheon proceeded, rounded off with a light dessert and cappucinos, their conversation ranged over a variety of subjects. Jill mentioned among other things her choral activities at St Wilfrid's, urging Marco to try and make his first-ever visit to Zurich for their annual, much-vaunted carol concert. Count Flavio reminisced about his childhood friendship with her mother among the Umbrian hills and made several references to his wife Amelia's artistic pursuits, of which he seemed very proud. Before they got up to leave, Count Flavio handed Jill a bulky Manila envelope, unsealed. Quickly checking its contents, the young woman placed it securely in her shoulder bag. None of the three diners paid any attention whatsoever to a gentleman in a corduroy jacket sitting two tables away from theirs and to all intents and purposes absorbed in a copy of *Time*, while also tackling a hearty lunch of meatballs and linguini.

"Have to get back to Stresa shortly, after attending to some matters here," Count Flavio said, as they reached the busy street outside the station. "Marco, who has Friday afternoons free, will drive you out to his school so that you can enjoy the views and look over the old place."

"That sounds wonderful," Jill said, with enthusiasm and a warm glance in Marco's direction. "But I shall have to be back in Bellinzona by 6.30 p.m., for my train."

With that, the count took his leave of them, with a request for Jill to convey his warmest regards to her mother. The music master then led his new companion two blocks to where his vintage Mini Cooper was parked. They were soon beyond the city limits, on the winding road into the hills, past small family farms, vineyards and rustic villages that seemed more than half-asleep.

"Count Flavio is a true patriot," Marco said, as the drive proceeded. "He's not happy at all with the way Europe is moving inexorably towards closer integration."

"You mean the new European Constitution and the push towards a federal state, like we have in America?"

"He could accept a free-trade area," Marco explained, "and the free movement of citizens across national borders, for work, study or any legitimate purpose."

"On the lines of the British approach?" she asked.

"The British are a very pragmatic people. They have little time for grandiose schemes and ideologies. That is their great strength. While joining in the EU, they are retaining their own currency, fiscal control and judicial powers. And who can blame them?"

Jill Crabtree pondered his remarks in silence, while taking in the picturesque views as the souped-up Mini rounded the sharp bends in the mountain road.

"And what is your opinion?" she asked, after a while.

"I agree with the count," Marco replied. "I don't care much at all for the concept of an integrated Europe and the uniformity that will inevitably result. Each European country has its own distinctive customs, traditions and language. It should remain that way. Whereas now, we have this amorphous Brussels bureaucracy imposing needless uniform regulations across all areas of European life."

"For example?" enquired the intrigued American, to whom this line of reasoning was refreshingly new. She had always tacitly assumed that most Europeans welcomed the idea of a united, and therefore stronger, Europe.

"What kinds of apples you can grow," the teacher said. "The content of sausages, the size of fish you can catch, the volume of sound an orchestra may make. You name it, and there's a regulation for it. Or, at any rate, there soon will be."

"But there must be some policies," Jill objected, "that will promote the common good. The environment, for example, or heath and safety issues."

"That may very well be," Marco countered. "But is that worth the trade-off in the loss of national independence and self-determination? Many groups across Europe do not think so, even if they are a distinct minority."

Jill Crabtree could not think of a ready answer to that and remained silent for the rest of the short drive to the gates of the school grounds. As they went through towards the parking lot, they passed students playing team games on the grassy pitches; others strolling around casually in smart burgundy blazers; yet others reading quietly in the shade of overhanging trees.

"Come," Marco said, as they alighted from the car. "I'll show you round the music department, then I'll introduce you to the principal, Fra Ignacio. After that, we'll take a walk through the grounds, followed by afternoon tea English-style, with muffins and strawberry jam and a pot of Earl Grey in the refectory. You'll love the paintings there."

The young American fell eagerly in step beside her unconventional guide, all thoughts of the European Union and its arcane problems receding from her mind.

⧓

As Jill Crabtree boarded the Milan-Zurich express in the early evening and occupied a window seat in the half-empty compartment, she reflected on what a delightful afternoon she had spent in the hills above Bellinzona. Marco Villanuova had turned out to be a most charming host and

guide, explaining how he organized his thriving department and introducing her to the school principal, Fra Ignacio. What an austere and arresting figure he had seemed
in his ankle-length black habit and small white bib, like a
French priest's. The Aurelian Brothers, he had explained,
had opened the school in the 1920s, to cater mainly for the
sons of Swiss and Italian diplomats and executives, whose
duties involved long absences overseas. A boarding school
in the Swiss alps seemed the most practical way of giving
their children continuity of education, rather than have
them accompany their parents around the globe, with the
constant disruption in schooling that would entail. Since
those early beginnings, the school had built on its growing reputation, drawing pupils from a much wider social
spectrum and preparing them for admission to the leading
universities of Europe and the USA.

As the express picked up speed towards the St Gotthard Tunnel, she drew the Manila envelope half out of her
shoulder bag and glanced at its contents. It contained large-
denomination Swiss banknotes. Intending to count it later
at her apartment, she quickly replaced the material, checking first that she remained unobserved. An uneasy thought
crossed her mind. What if she were getting into something
above her head? When it had been proposed to her that she
make this trip to Ticino, she had been more than a little
surprised when informed that she was to meet with Count
Flavio de Montesedina. In the circumstances, she could
hardly refuse, given the close family and business connections of the Italian aristocrat with both her parents. Never
having personally met him, this seemed an opportune way
to do so and, in the event, she was very pleased at the encounter, since she could give her mother good reports of
his health and well-being. As to his views, eccentric as they
appeared they were shared in large part, she well knew, by

her own mother. It was mainly out of loyalty to her that she had agreed to this dubious venture. She was to disguise the money as part of the International School fund. As bursar and registrar, she would have little difficulty in doing this, having oversight of the school accounts. She had also been assured that this irregular arrangement was to be of short duration, and she had agreed to it on that basis only, considering the doubtful provenance of the large sum involved. On the other hand, she had no reason at all to question the count's integrity. In fact, the reverse was true.

Still the feeling of unease persisted, as the express hurtled into the long, dark tunnel. When it finally emerged into the pale evening light over central Switzerland and its steep, wooded valleys, her preoccupations had switched emphasis. She fell to wondering about her relationship with Max Fifield, whom she had known for several years. Their friendship had developed up to a point, but no further. Perhaps this was so, she felt, because the book representative was so much part of the choir group and preferred to organize his social life around them, in group activities such as restaurant evenings, orchestral concerts at the Tonhalle and day trips to places of interest; and in the winter months he ventured into the mountains most weekends with Hugh Selby. Both she and Margaret Fern had proved unable to master the difficult art of downhill skiing.

If she saw her romantic future linked with Max Fifield, it was slow in developing, and the uneasy thought crossed her mind that he might not be the marrying kind. His bachelor life in Zurich seemed so complete and fulfilling. Yet they had enjoyed a close friendship apart from the group; and she thought she had read evidence, occasional though it might have been, of a genuine affection on his part. Unless it was that curious phenomenon called cupboard love that she had experienced before back in Boston: the dependency of the lone male on creature comforts such as home cooking and small personal services like laundry and ironing shirts. Perish the thought, she considered, if that was all it amounted to. As the train sped through Schwyz, the last main station on the Zurich line, her thoughts switched to Marco Villanuova, the handsome and personable young music master at Collegio San Isidoro, whom she estimated to be several years her junior. It pleased her more than she cared to admit that he had promised to attend the Kantorei concert at the Tonhalle in August, as well as St Wilfrid's carol service in December.

chapter 5

FIRST THING MONDAY morning, while enjoying his breakfast in the dining-room of Hotel Fiedler, in company with a tourist from New Zealand who had been placed opposite him for want of a free table, George Mason received a telephone call from Leutnant Rolf Kubler. Without going into details over the line, the Swiss officer implied that there were interesting developments following Kaporal Goetz's tailing of Jill Crabtree on Friday. He invited the detective to meet him over lunch at Restaurant zum Wildhaus on the Uetliberg and gave him detailed directions on how to find it. Mason noted them carefully. He was to go to the Hauptbahnhof and locate the funicular railway at the far end of the concourse, well apart from the regular trains. It was a frequent service that would take him to the top of the ridge running along the southern side of the valley, giving panoramic views of the city and the lake below. On alighting from the train, he was to proceed about two hundred yards along the densely-wooded path to reach the Wildhaus. The lieutenant would expect him there around midday.

"Duty calls," Mason said, rising from his place and taking leave of his table companion, an agreeable young man doing a European tour. "Are you going sight-seeing today?"

"Opting for a cruise down the lake, as far as Rapperswil," the New Zealander said. "Do you happen to know where the boat departs?"

"From the far end of the Bahnhofstrasse," Mason advised. "Cross over the dual-carriageway there and you'll find the boat quay directly opposite."

He soon stepped out into the bright morning sunshine and, with a couple of hours to spare, reassumed his adopted role of package-tour scout, crossing the stone bridge over the Limmat to reach the Munsterhof. He discovered a large medieval square open to the river on one side and lined on the remaining three by buildings in pale-colored stone that gave it an air of timeless elegance. On one hand stood a large guildhall; on the other, the imposing Liebfrauenkirche. Since the guildhall was not open to the public, he opted for the famous church, joining the handful of visitors already inside admiring the vaulted nave and the impressive stained-glass windows of strikingly-modern design. A stone tablet set into the wall of the narthex informed him that the building had offered sanctuary to hundreds of Huguenots, those Protestants who fled France following the Massacre of St Bartholomew's Eve in the late-1600s, thousands of whose co-religionists had, he recalled reading somewhere, made their way to welcoming English shores.

A short distance from the Munsterhof, along the narrow, winding alleys of the Altstadt, the oldest part of the city that had formed the nucleus of the Roman Turicum, he came across a secluded square fringed with linden trees and bordered on one side by the austere lines of the Peterkirche. He sat down on a bench to light a small cigar, while just catching the strains of an organist practicing a Bach fugue within. On the stroke of eleven, his attention was arrested by the pealing of bells from its impressive tower with the large painted clock, one of the characteristic landmarks of this ancient city. He checked his watch; it synchronized to within a few seconds. He would finish his cigar and enjoy the organ recital in the broad sunshine, the seagulls wheeling overhead, as an unexpected perk of this intriguing assignment. Chief Inspector Harrington would just about now be having his usual tot of Glenfiddich along with his morning coffee. Good luck to him, the detective thought. In weather like this, no desk in Whitehall, not even the superintendant's, could compare in his mind with a simple wooden bench in Zurich's Peterhof.

He was fifteen minutes late at the Restaurant zum Wildhaus, being loathe to leave his seat before the end of the organ performance. Rolf Kubler rose from his place by a leaded rear window to greet him, as George Mason found himself in a rustic interior of pinewood furniture and floral curtains, with a stag's antlers above the hearth and a stuffed lynx on the mantlepiece. The establishment was barely half full.

"Have a seat," the lieutenant said, indicating the chair opposite his and handing him the menu. "So you found me at last."

"Sorry to keep you waiting," Mason apologized. "Just missed the funicular at the Hauptbahnhof. Had to wait twenty minutes for the next one."

"Thought you might enjoy the view," Kubler said, seemingly happy to introduce his English counterpart to attractions off the beaten track.

Mason sensed, however, that the remote venue was more for the lieutenant's benefit than his own; but he was inwardly pleased, since it would never have occurred to him to take the funicular railway, with the wonderful bird's-eye view it gave of the city and the surrounding countryside. He nodded in agreement and briefly scanned the menu.

58

"You implied there were developments at Bellinzona," he remarked, placing an order for meatballs and pasta with the young brunette dressed in traditional dirndl partly obscured by a pale-blue apron. Not quite Heidi, he thought, conjuring in his mind the stereotypical image of a blond Swiss teenager with pigtails.

"Goetz easily identified the American woman from the photograph you took for us," the Swiss replied, when the waitress was out of earshot.

"And?" prompted Mason.

"Dressed as a Tyrolean he managed, without arousing their suspicion, to occupy a table close to where she took lunch with two Italians. He caught only brief snatches of the conversation, but he thought the general drfit was anti-European."

"That's very interesting," Mason observed. "Max Fifield holds strong anti-European views. Or at least he did so in the recent past."

"Jill Crabtree took off somewhere by car with the younger man shortly after the meal. Goetz could not follow them and has no idea where they went."

"He caught the next train back to Zurich?"

"Only after tailing the older man for a while, apparently to no purpose, round bookshops and artists' suppliers, where he purchased small tubes of paint."

"Is that all we have, then?" the deflated detective asked, turning his attention to the platter of meatballs, at the same time ordering a German beer.

"By no means," Kubler retorted, a glint of triumph in his eye. "A large Manila envelope changed hands in the course of the meal. It was given by the older Italian to the American."

"Does your corporal have any idea what it contained?"

"He seemed pretty sure," the Swiss replied, "that it held banknotes. The envelope wasn't sealed and the American glanced briefly at the contents before placing it in her shoulder bag."

George Mason tackled his appetizing lunch thoughtfully, with occasional sips of his Paulaner Export, as Rolf Kubler tucked into his cutlets and brown rice with gusto, determined to make the most of his luncheon in the wilds of Uetliberg. Suddenly recalling the information Franz Hassler had given him on Lake Lucerne, Mason asked:

"Where would someone put a large sum of money like that, supposing it was tainted? Could advantage be taken of your notorious banking secrecy laws?"

"Not if criminality is suspected," the Swiss responded, emphatically.

"So she would probably not place it in a bank account?"

"She would certainly risk exposure," Kubler said, "if there's a question of legitimacy. But aren't you rather jumping to conclusions?"

Mason, ignoring that last remark, finished his meal in silence and sat back to relish his beer, impressed at the excellent appetite of his companion, while declining his offer of apfel strudel for dessert. He was thinking, as usual, of his waistline.

"How difficult would it be to examine the accounts of the International School," he asked suddenly, "without arousing suspicion?"

Kubler almost spilled his tankard of brown ale at the unexpectedness of the question.

"What kind of a proposition is that?" he asked, testily.

"Before Jill Crabtree came to Zurich three years ago," the detective explained, "she held a similar post at a school in Freiburg. I have it on good authority that, during her tenure there, some irregularities were found in the school accounts."

Rolf Kubler pushed his plate aside and pondered Mason's remark for a few moments, in the hiatus between courses. After a while, he said:

"If you're really serious about this, we can arrange for a special audit by the Kantonal Taxburo. These take place from time to time at Swiss enterprises, without prior warning. A kind of spot check, if you like, to counteract fraud and money laundering."

"Sounds like a good system," Mason remarked. "How soon can you put it in hand?"

"Within days, if the request comes through the police department."

The lieutenant's strudel arrived, fully occupying his attention, as George Mason finished his beer, glanced round at the other occupants of the restaurant and admired the rustic décor, thinking that something similar might only be found in Britain in the remoter Cairngorms, in the wilderness of northern Scotland.

"By the way," Kubler said, his appetite fully satisfied, "I'm afraid there's another theft to report."

"Which book this time?" Mason enquired.

"Not a book, but a music manuscript. The piano score of Mozart's opera *Don Giovanni* has gone missing from the Winterthur Institute of Fine Arts. It's the first published edition from the 1790s, rather than the composer's handwritten manuscript, but still worth a considerable sum of money."

"Winterthur?" quizzed a puzzled Mason.

"A university town about thirty miles north of here," Kubler said, checking his watch.

"Let's discuss it on the walk back to the station. Must be back at my desk by two o'clock at the latest, for the weekly briefing."

With that, he summoned the waitress, settled the bill and led his English counterpart out of The Wildhaus, pointing out as they regained the path some interesting features on the far side of the valley, known as the Zurichberg.

"These thefts of books and manuscripts," Mason observed, "seem to be quite a regular occurrence."

"Taking Europe as a whole," Kubler informed him, "hundreds, if not thousands, of items disappear from libraries every year. Often enough, the staff are not aware that they are missing until many months later. It's a serious problem."

"And where do these items finish up?" Mason wanted to know.

"In private and even public collections in America and the Far East," the other replied. "Even though there are laws in place to protect a nation's cultural heritage, not all museums, antiquarians and dealers abroad observe them too strictly."

"You mean they don't always fully check the status and provenance of the items they acquire?" Mason asked, in some surprise.

"Exactly so. Compliance with the guidelines drawn up by UNESCO is voluntary, so many institutions turn a blind eye when it comes to high-value collectibles. They're so keen to own them."

"I've read in the newspapers," Mason said, "of court cases by survivors of the Holocaust or by descendants of victims to get museums and art galleries to return paintings stolen from them during World War 11. And there's the ongoing case in England of the Elgin Marbles from the Acropolis, demanded back by Greece."

62

"Those are the high-profile cases," Kubler told him, as they reached the train station to watch the twin-car funicular slowly scale the steep valley side, " the ones that get into the press. Taking rare books, art, sculptures and archaeological treasures all together, the problem is quite phenomenal."

"But you are doing your bit to stem this trade in Switzerland," the detective said, with approval.

"And you are doing *your* bit to help us," Rolf Kubler quipped, with evident satisfaction.

As the train pulled into Uetliberg Station and discharged its few passengers, the two police officers boarded it and contented themselves with the stunning views on the descent. They parted company, almost like old friends, when they reach the terminus.

Margaret Fern rose early that day, took a quick shower, dressed and prepared a simple repast of cottage cheese and rye bread in her small, compact kitchen. She felt very pleased to have found this accommodation in what was known as the English Quarter of Zurich. She occupied a small bed-sitting room with balcony in a large apartment shared by four other professional young women. The kitchen and adjoining dining-room were communal areas, allowing for a degree of social intercourse among the occupants, usually in the snatched hours between work and sleep; and at weekends among those who remained in the city rather than visit family, as some of them often did, in different parts of the country. By 8.00 a.m., she was ready to quit the apartment and hurry to the tram stop to catch the Number 15 for her twenty-five minute journey to the industrial suburb of Oerlikon, where Succor occupied a small suite of offices in a converted shoe factory. It was not the most elegant business address in Zurich, but quite adequate for their purposes as a leading charitable organization. Her employment there was not well-remunerated, barely covering her living expenses and allowing just a small margin of savings, which she used for annual trips to England. But it had a high degree of job satisfaction.

As she sat in the modern tram on its smooth glide towards the city center, she felt particularly heartened by the project currently in hand, a hostel they were establishing in Debrecen, a medium-sized town north-east of Budapest, as a safe house and staging post for East European girls who had escaped the clutches of sex traffickers. It had become one of her pet schemes since joining the staff of the charity two years ago, following the post-graduate certificate in social work she had pursued at York University in her mid-twenties after an unsuccessful foray into school teaching. She sympathized with the plight of young girls caught up in the upheavals of the last several years in the Balkans and elsewhere. Most of them were lured abroad by tempting, but bogus offers of employment as waitresses, store assistants, domestics and the like; only to be ensnared in the international sex trade. Issued with false passports and visas, they were sold on to minders who ruthlessly exploited them, forcing them to work long hours to pay off their purchase price and threatening them with violence if they attempted to contact the police. It was a modern form of slavery extremely difficult to escape.

The tram negotiated the busy junction by the Hauptbahnhof and picked up speed on the more open stretch towards Oerlikon. She would make the office in time, she considered, feeling a sense of relief that her associate Laszlo was taking one of his allotted vacation days. She had been concerned for some weeks now about the slow progress being made on the Debrecen hostel, despite the sizeable funds allocated to it by the director, Signore Pollini, who had been sent up from headquarters in Perugia to manage the Zurich office. Her first task that day would be to raise the matter with Pollini, since it was Laszlo who had overall responsibility for projects in East Europe, being himself of Hungarian descent. Adept at European languages, he made occasional visits to former socialist countries and managed the appropriate funds. He was also a bachelor and, if the rumor-mill was credible, something of a Don Juan.

With five more stops to go, she took out the score of Mozart's *Mass in C* they were scheduled to sing at the Tonhalle at the end of August and softly hummed the alto line of the *Kyrie*, the only section they had so far covered, to refresh her memory of last week's rehearsal. Membership of the Kantorei was one of the highlights of her life in Zurich. It was a large mixed choir, much more ambitious in scope than St Wilfrid's, that gave two public performances each year in the main concert hall facing the lake. Possessing only moderate musical ability, she had been very gratified when the conductor, following a brief audition, had assigned her a place among the altos. It was up to her, she felt, to justify his confidence by practicing hard before each performance, to make sure that she was, as nearly as possible, note-perfect.

She was aware, too, that Max Fifield set great store by their membership of the Kantorei, seeing in it a reflection of their competence as church singers with their own established reputation stemming mainly from the annual carol concert. Max and Jill invariably arrived together for the rehearsals and, although they seemed very close, their relationship did not appear to her to have developed beyond a certain point. If she herself had romantic ambitions in his regard, she tended to suppress them. Max was certainly eligible, with passable good looks without being strikingly handsome, a good job in publishing and an air of self-assurance she at times found slightly irritating. Hugh Selby, on the other hand, was younger than she and not quite ready, in her opinion, to form serious attachments. And now there was this new addition to St Wilfrid's in the shape of George Mason. A stroke of luck that he possessed a useful bass, to strengthen the men's section. But what an odd sort of person he seemed, to have turned up in their midst just like that. He didn't strike her at all as having a background in tourism; but it took all sorts, as her mother was fond of saying, to make a world. If he seemed to her more like a customs officer or a tax inspector or something official like that, it may just have been a superficial impression. George was certainly good company, with his interesting anecdotes and wry sense of humor.

⌘

Laszlo Polke slept later than usual, having arranged to take one of his allotted vacation days. He sublet one room in a large apartment on the second floor of Heldenstrasse 2, not far from the university and almost exactly opposite the residence occupied by the Irish novelist James Joyce in the thirties, marked by a small blue plaque set into the outside wall. On rising, he made his way to the communal bathroom he shared with three other subtenants at the end of a long, dim corridor, to wash and shave. His fellow tenants had long since left for work and, in any case, he rarely met them. They were all much older than he, middle-aged bachelors who returned each evening to the privacy of their rooms. They greeted him curtly, usually with little more than a nod, if he passed them on the narrow corridor, paid their rent regularly to the apartment owner, Frau Genucchi, and generally kept to themselves, receiving no visitors that he was aware of. Occasionally, through the thin walls, he would catch the sound of his immediate neighbor's television set or a recording of traditional jazz.

Since Frau Genucchi, an elderly widow from Ticino, did not share her kitchen with the subtenants, as soon as he was dressed he went down to the Culman, a medium-sized restaurant on the ground floor of the apartment building, to take his customary light breakfast of milk coffee and croissants. At 9.30 in the morning it was virtually empty of its usual clientele of office girls, shop assistants and clerks, apartment dwellers like himself who dropped in on their way to work. Having placed his order, he occupied a window table, flicked through the pages of *Tages Anzeiger* and glanced occasionally at the trams picking up speed on the steep descent down Ramistrasse towards Belle Vue. Glancing at his watch, he decided he had ample time to catch the 10.55 a.m. *Schnellzug* to Lausanne. The long flight of stone steps just behind the restaurant would lead him down to the Hauptbahnhof in about fifteen minutes.

A trip to Lausanne, a beautiful city on the shores of Lake Geneva, would combine business with pleasure. He would book a leisurely afternoon cruise to take full advantage of the spring sunshine, disembark at Montreux for an early dinner on one of the hotel terraces perched over the water, with stirring views of the snow-capped alps, before catching the evening train back to Zurich. Completing his brief repast, he withdrew his wallet to make sure that he had not forgotten the Succor check in favor of Tomas Vasaryk. His main task that day was to deposit it in the account kept by Vasaryk at Balaton Bank. It was the first East European finance house to open a branch in Switzerland following the collapse of Communism, and it was noted for its exceptional discretion in handling transactions for its customers, many of them Hungarian entrepreneurs seeking business openings in the West.

His main concern was whether his colleague Margaret Fern suspected anything. With oversight of East European projects, he had appointed on his own authority Tomas Vasaryk as one of sub-contractors for the Debrecen hostel for young women. Part of the monies transferred to Vasaryk were being siphoned off to a secret account in Budapest kept by Zeged, an ultra-nationalist organization opposed to both globalization and membership of the European Union, on the grounds that they undermined national traditions and identity. Margaret Fern had of late begun to prod him about slow progress on a project close to her heart and it concerned him that she might have raised the matter behind his back with Signore Pollini. If challenged by the charity's director, he would blame local suppliers and labor disputes, both of them quite plausible reasons, for the unexpected delays.

Laszlo Polke was, in his own eyes, a true patriot dedicated to the future of Hungary as an independent nation-state. The movement among his compatriots to join the EU was, he felt, largely due to pressure from business interests who anticipated greater profits from membership of the Common Market. They would willingly sacrifice the country's independence to their own narrow agenda. As he went for a refill of coffee and pushed the newspaper aside, he felt fully justified in taking risks in support of the nationalists. Hungary had, after all, barely broken free of the Soviet yoke, and it was not many decades since it had emerged from the dominion of Austria after World War 1. To merge its identity now within a greater Europe was inconceivable and it must not be allowed to happen. Zeged was the only organization he knew of capable of rousing public opinion in sufficient volume against it, before the planned referendum took place. Zeged meant 'fortress' in English, an entirely appropriate name, in Laszlo's view.

As he settled his bill and began the long descent to the station, his thoughts were on his father and the sacrifices he had been forced to make. He recalled how Andreas Polke, originally from Szob, a town just north-west of Budapest, had as a teenager taken part in the Uprising of 1956, fleeing across the border into Austria as the Russian tanks moved in, leaving his aged parents behind. Eventually moving to Switzerland, his engineering qualifications were not fully recognized and the best employment he could obtain was maintaining and repairing ski-lifts in the small resorts of the Arlberg Pass, not too far from Zurich, where he raised his family. They had lived in modest circumstances in a crowded apartment building well away from the lake and the expensive amenities of the inner city. Laszlo himself had matriculated from the local gynasium and proceeded to Stuttgart University to study Slavonic languages. His second-class degree eventually landed him a job at a leading charity, providing him with a basic standard of living that left little scope for luxuries. Material comforts, however, were far from his idealistic mind as he entered the spacious concourse of the Hauptbahnhof to join the short queue at the ticket office.The Zurich-Geneva express, calling at Bern and Lausanne, was just pulling into Platfrom 10.

chapter 6

MAX FIFIELD ROSE on Tuesday morning anticipating his meeting that day with the secretary of the Britannia Party. Keith Kendall would be passing through Zurich on his way by car from St Moritz, where he had been taking a late-season winter sports vacation in the southern alps. Since he would be heading north to call on his one European Parliament member in Strasbourg before proceeding to Paris, it had been agreed by telephone that Max would accompany him as far as Schaffhausen on the German border, since the secretary was particularly keen to visit the scenic Rhine Falls there. The arrangement suited Max, who had book business at the city's polytechnic. They were to meet mid-morning at Belle Vue and drive to Regenswil, a picturesque village in an area of the upper Rhine noted for its white wines, where they would take lunch at the Restaurant zum Reben.

The sky had clouded over as he left his apartment near the Kunsthaus and commenced walking the half-mile or so down Ramistrasse towards the lake, hoping that the rain would hold off at least until they had reached their destination. He was a little concerned too that the party secretary, unaccustomed to the growing tourist traffic, might not make it in time from his overnight stop in Chur. That was a chance he would have to take, he reflected, as he reached the busy intersection facing the Opera House to occupy a pavement table at the celebrated Gruene Heinrich restaurant, so-named after a prominent character in Swiss fiction. He ordered lemon tea, which he generally preferred to coffee as being more English, flicked through the pages of *Tages Anzeiger* and cast an occasional eye on the clouds building over the distant mountains.

Jill's assignation at Bellinzona had gone according to plan. What a stroke of luck it had been to discover, in the course of casual conversation with her over dinner at her apartment, that she had family connections with Count Flavio de Montesedina. It had taken a little persuasion on his part to enlist her support, which was eventually achieved by representing it as a means of assisting the Italian aristocrat in an important project. He sensed too that he had some influence over her, partly as leader of the choir group and partly as close friend in the time they shared away from the others. To some degree, also, he felt protective of her and had some qualms at the possibility of compromising her in any way.

He only went ahead with the scheme in the knowledge that she had complete control of the school budget and that the arrangements he had put in place were to be of relatively short duration. Suddenly glancing up from his newspaper, he spotted the sprightly figure of Keith Kendall waiting for a pedestrian signal to permit him to cross from the middle of the large tram station. Jay-walking incurred spot-fines.

Max Fifield rose to greet him as he successfully negotiated the busy junction.

"Sorry I'm a bit late," Kendall said, grasping the other's palm in a vigorous handshake. "Traffic, mainly German skiers judging by car number plates, was heavier than I expected. And there was a roadworks just outside Landquart."

"Where are you parked?" Fifield enquired.

"Down by the lake, just opposite the Wienerwald."

The two men walked a short distance up Seefeldstrasse, where they could cross more easily near the Opera House, and were soon seated inside a vintage Jaguar with leather upholstery. They headed north out of the city and into the rolling, lightly-wooded countryside beyond, as the secretary recounted the highlights of his holiday.

"I suppose you have been kept quite busy with your new job," he remarked, eventually. "What is it exactly that you do here?"

"I represent a publisher of academic books," Max informed him. "On the road quite a lot, visiting universities, polytechnics and colleges."

"It was a good move," Kendall said, "in view of our poor showing at the last election. We currently have only two MPs at Westminster and one member of the European Parliament."

"I'm surprised that you should want representation in Strasbourg," Max said, "given the party's views on European union."

"Better to influence things from within, rather than from the outside," the other offered, in justification. "There'll be a general election in two years' time, if not before. Do you intend returning to Milcaster to take up your old post as party organiser?"

Max pondered the idea for a while, glancing out of the side window at the passing scenery, the small farms and villages with half-timbered buildings that were such an attractive feature of the Zurich Oberland.

"That very much depends on how things turn out here," he said. "I've made some useful contacts with people of similar convictions and fund-raising activities are doing quite well. There may well be significant developments in the short term."

"I hope it's all above board," Kendall stressed. "No money-laundering or anything of that kind. If the British press linked the Britannia Party to devious activities, they'd have a field day. It would set us back a generation."

The book salesman fell silent again, as he watched for road signs to Regenswil and the scheduled lunch stop. Curious, he thought, that his companion should be so squeamish. In his own mind, the end fully justified the means and there was no way they were going to achieve their objective of distancing Britain from Europe through normal electoral processes. And now there was all this talk of a new European Constitution, a step on the way to creating a unified, federal state. His country should take no part in it and concentrate instead on its ties with the Commonwealth, those fifty or so countries spread across the globe that shared British values and acknowledged the Queen.

"Pull off the road about a hundred yards ahead," he instructed, to give his driver time to reduce speed, "straight onto the Reben parking lot."

"Will do," Kendall replied, applying the breaks and easing the powerful sedan into the restricted space beside the restaurant.

They climbed out and strolled to the edge of the lot to take in the view down the steep valley side, to where the Rhine, quite narrow at this point on its journey to the North Sea, meandered unhurriedly below, reflecting glints of bright sunshine through gaps in the clouds. Max felt glad that the rain had held off.

"I can recommend either the grilled trout or the coq-au-vin," he said, from experience, as they stepped inside a rustic restaurant with décor suggestive of the local wine industry. "The white wines are very distinctive and well worth sampling."

"I'll defer to your good judgment," the secretary said, as they chose a table aside from the other guests and promptly placed their order for river trout.

While awaiting service, he brought Max Fifield up to date on news and developments back home: how they were aiming to field extra candidates at the next elections; the shape of party finances and the minor scandal involving one of their agents caught in a love triangle. The salesman took it all in eagerly enough, thinking there was plenty of time before deciding whether to take part in a future election. For one thing, it would mean giving up the congenial life-style he had developed in Zurich and his involvement with St Wilfrid's choir and the Kantorei; not to mention the close friendships he had cultivated. Once served, they concentrated on eating their meal, taking to the road again in good time to visit the tourist sites before Max's appointment at the polytechnic.

"Keep in touch about any developments," Keith Kendall advised him, as an hour later they took their parting glance at the broad sweep of the Rhine across the famous falls.

"Will do," Max promised, as they left the viewing platform and walked towards the parked car, where he shook hands with his companion and watched him drive away before directing his steps towards the center of Schaffhausen and the polytechnic.

Erik Muntener was one of several student contacts he had unofficially made at the various colleges in his sales territory. As insiders, they had full access to student facilities, including libraries and specialist collections such as historical documents and records, that were not available to the general public. Since they were trusted members of their respective communities, it was a simple enough procedure to obtain a key to those glass-fronted cabinets where rarer materials were displayed.

Max Fifield strode confidently across the main square towards the pavement tables of the Restaurant zum Goldenen Hind, sat down and ordered a lager beer to refresh himself after his journey. The pedestrianized central square was only moderately busy at this early-afternoon hour, with groups of students crossing from the bus station to the nearby polytechnic and shoppers moving in and out of department stores and boutiques. Thinking at first that Erik had been delayed at a lecture or tutorial, he grew quite concerned when, by three o'clock, the young student had still failed to appear. Time was now against him, as he had an appointment at 3.15 p.m. with the chairman of the Department of Computer Studies, to present Manfred Bott AG's latest publications in the field of software design.

On the supposition that the thief or thieves might be looking for a quick turnover, George Mason had spent that morning visiting second-hand bookshops on the Neumarkt and the steep, cobbled alleys off the Bahnhofstrasse, in the hope of discovering the final destination of the stolen books. After a fruitless three hours and a quick lunch of cervelats, a type of sausage he smothered in French mustard, he made his way towards the Polizei Dienst in response to Leutnant Rolf Kubler's request for an early meeting. The young visitor from New Zealand had moved on, to make his way in stages down the Rhine as far as Cologne, leaving the detective sole occupant of his dining-room table, from where he could overhear the excited chatter of a family group from Canada, who had checked into the Fiedler at the weekend.

"Have a seat," the lieutenant offered, as Mason entered the rather cramped premises just as an orderly was clearing away a luncheon tray. "Had a useful morning?"

"Only in the sense of ruling things out," Mason replied, a touch ruefully. "Must have called at half a dozen bookshops and drawn a blank each time. A fascinating experience, even so."

"If you're that fond of old books," the other remarked, dryly. "The goods in question could be anywhere by now, even on the other side of the world."

George Mason eased his portly frame into a chair facing his Swiss counterpart and waited patiently, glad to be off his feet, as several quick phone calls were made, papers were shuffled and files replaced in cabinets. Rolf Kubler evidently had a lot on his plate. Having cleared the decks, as it were, he now gave his English visitor full attention.

"Some news for you regarding your friend, Jill Crabtree," he began, as George Mason leaned forward attentively. "Acting on your suggestion, we arranged for the Kantonal Taxburo to do a special audit of her school accounts."

"And you turned something up?" Mason immediately asked.

"There are certainly irregularities," Kubler continued, "if rather puzzling ones."

"Puzzling?" the detective queried. "What exactly do you mean?"

Leutnant Kubler cleared his throat.

"Normally," he said, "a special audit will reveal irregularities such as embezzlement, cooking the books, or other forms of what might best be described as creative accounting. In this case, however, there appear to be more funds on the school books than can be allowed for by students' fees, donations and endowments."

"Endowments?"

"Monies placed in trust, usually by former alumni, to boost the income from students' fees, garden fetes and the like."

"That's most interesting," the detective observed. "So where do we go from here?"

"That very much depends on you," Kubler replied. "Jill Crabtree can hardly be charged with embezzlement."

"What about money laundering?"

"In that case," the Swiss explained, "we would need to know more about the supply side. All we have to go off is an elderly Italian gentleman who made a short visit to Bellinzona, to have lunch with Jill Crabtree and purchase art supplies."

George Mason fell silent for a while, pondering this new information and its possible implications.

"We need to do more research," he said, eventually.

"On the other hand," Kubler said, "we could pull her in for questioning. Find out who her Italian contact is and what this—how shall I best describe it?—reverse embezzlement is all about."

"That might be premature," Mason replied. "At least until we know more about the purloined books, which did not originate in Italy. If you bring Ms Crabtree in now for a grilling, that may merely serve to alert any other parties that may be involved. I'd sit on this information for the time being, until some related evidence turns up."

The Swiss officer gave his counterpart a questioning look, as if undecided about the wisdom of that line of procedure. He decided in the end to give the Englishman the benefit of the doubt.

"I'll buy that for the time being," he said, "pending your further enquiries."

"Have you anything else to report?"

"As a matter of fact, I have," the lieutenant replied. "This morning I received a visit from a Signore Pollini, director of a leading charity called Succor."

"Indeed?" responded Mason, much intrigued. "I in fact know someone who works for them. Succor exists to rescue women from the sex trade and from domestic abuse."

"A most worthy cause," Kubler agreed, "deserving of our full support. Signore Pollini, however, suspects that a member of his staff is misdirecting funds earmarked for a hostel project in Hungary."

"That person wouldn't by any chance be a certain Margaret Fern, would it?" the detective enquired, anxiously. "She sings alto in our choir."

"On the contrary, it's a young male member of the staff, named Laszlo Polke. Pollini has asked us to look into the matter, find out what we can about his background and activities. I'm putting Alfons Goetz onto it straight away."

"Let me know at once if he turns up something," Mason said. "It may or may not be linked to Jill Crabtree's irregular accounting practices."

As George Mason left police premises, crossed over the Bahnhofplatz and made his way thoughtfully along the Limmatquai, he felt a sense of unease that Margaret Fern, as well as Jill Crabtree, could be linked, however tenuously, to some form of financial chicanery. Was it mere coincidence that all roads seemed to be leading, if not to Rome, as the Catholic writer Hilaire Belloc was fond of saying, then to St Wilfrid's church? And what about Max Fifield? Where did he fit into all this, as acknowledged leader of the group. Was the reputable church choir, in fact, a hive of intrigue?

Choir practice had been moved forward a day so that Dr Hurlimann could attend a conductors' conference at Lugano. George Mason, after resting up in his hotel room following his exertions that morning visiting second-hand bookshops, emerged again in the early evening. Since the clouds had cleared, after threatening rain, he had in mind an early outdoor dinner before trekking up Ramistrasse to reach the church in good time. Negotiating the narrow alley that led from his hotel to the embankment, he crossed the river near the Wasserkirche and made his way along the opposite bank to a large garden restaurant, ideally situated at the point where the Limmat flowed out from the lake. It was a self-service, just now beginning to fill up with early diners like himself. Grabbing a tray, he made his way along the counter, chose one of the warm pasta dishes and found a table near the perimeter, whence he could observe the yachts tacking across the water and the river boats ferrying tourists. Gulls wheeled noisily overhead and made occasional swoops for easy pickings from the restaurant tables. The food, a spaghetti Bolognese, was one of his favorite pastas and he treated himself to a glass of merlot to go with it. He would gladly have lingered there until dark, when the fairy lights went on and a trio played music for dancing. He had caught strains at times through the open window of his hotel room.

But duty called. He reached St Wilfrid's just before seven and took his accustomed place among the handful of basses, feeling now more confident of his notes as the anthem for Pentecost began to take more robust shape. The dim interior of the hallowed building, the flair of the silver-haired conductor and the dedication of the choristers as they proceeded *a cappella* through the Vaughan Williams score seemed light years away from the aura of mystery and intrigue that, in the detective's mind, was beginning to envelop this small, rather esoteric, community. He glanced more than once in the direction of Jill Crabtree, prominent among the sopranos; and at Margaret Fern in the altos. Hugh Selby did sterling work with the tenors. Afterwards, just before nine o'clock, they repaired to Der Waldman for their usual nightcap.

"So what have you dug up to tempt the British tourists?" Margaret wanted to know at once, as they occupied their accustomed table in the rustic *Stube*, which was almost full of clients.

The detective felt at a loss, having concentrated most of his energies on visiting second-hand bookshops. He thought quickly.

"I've been up the Uetliberg," he replied, inventively. "And to the zoo. I've also priced the excursions on the lake boats and sampled a few of the restaurants."

"So you've been enjoying yourself," Hugh Selby quipped, "while we're all slaving away at work. Such fine weather, too."

"If you're interested in cultural events," Margaret said, "you should check out the Pergolesi Festival. The setting for it is quite wonderful."

"And where would that be?" Mason asked, intrigued.

"In the southern alps, above Bellinzona," she replied, enthusiastically. "I went there for the first time last year, when my mother visited."

"Doesn't that take place in the grounds of a school?" Max Fifield asked.

"At the Collegio San Isidoro," Jill Crabtree put in, without mentioning her recent trip there with Marco. "This year they're putting on an opera, *The Maid as Mistress*."

"I enjoy open-air opera performances," Mason said, thinking back to the Gilbert and Sullivan evenings in the grounds of Gawsworth Hall in Cheshire. "I'll certainly look into it. Thanks for the useful tip."

Not to be outdone, Max Fifield said: "You should also take in the Rhine Falls at Schaffhausen. It's the sort of thing tourists generally go for, and not all that well-known to most Britons."

"They're more likely to visit Niagara," Hugh Selby observed, dryly.

"The Rhine Falls are by no means as spectacular," the salesman explained, "but still well worth seeing. I was there myself only this afternoon, having business at the polytechnic."

"I can see I'll have lots of good ideas for Bowland Tours," Mason said, maintaining his pretence, "thanks to all your helpful suggestions."

He felt ill at ease deceiving these well-meaning people in this way; yet on the other hand he had an important job to do. Chief Inspector Harrington wouldn't give him any credit for scruples.

They chatted on pleasantly for the next hour, about this and that, but mainly about routine parish affairs that were not of much concern to him, until the cuckoo clock on the wall announced the hour of ten. They then summoned the waitress and settled their accounts. As they parted company on the street outside, the detective noticed that Max and Jill again walked off together in one direction, while Hugh and Margaret parted and took different routes. He himself headed back towards the Niederdorf, the center of the city's night-life, with its cafes, cinemas and clubs in full swing and the long, narrow street leading through it crammed with visitors. He considered, as he strolled along towards his hotel, his nostrils regaled by the odor of grilled bratwurst from the street vendors and his ears assailed by pop music or jazz through open doorways, that it had been quite an interesting day.

chapter 7

FRA CELESTINO AWOKE just after sunrise on Wednesday morning, donned his ankle-length black habit and joined the small community of Aurelian Brothers in the school grounds for a half-hour of meditation, strolling across the tailored lawns overhung with cedar trees in a silence disturbed only by the dawn chorus. With wispy white hair, he was well into his seventies, a member of the small group of lay brothers who did no teaching, but were responsible for maintaining the fabric of the property and the extensive grounds, which included a large apple orchard abutting dense woods. He had particular responsibility for storing the apples and distributing one each to the students after supper, when they had their final outdoor recreation before bed. He had spent most of his working life at San Isisdoro's and had no thoughts of retiring to the Brothers' rest home in the Engadin, preferring to remain an active member of the community until the very end, should his superiors permit.

After the short period of meditation, a bell summoned them to the school chapel. Celestino followed slowly after his confreres as they silently filed into the pews and began on the stroke of seven to chant the morning office. They were accustomed by now to hearing his shrill voice sing loudly off-key from the plainsong score in their breviaries, but that did not unduly distract them as they proceeded from long custom through the order of service to the final Latin stanza: *ecce quam bonum et quam iucundum, fratres habitare in unum*—how good and pleasant it is for brothers to live as one. One of the pleasantest aspects, to the lay brother's mind, was the American-style cooked breakfast they then enjoyed in the school refectory, a hearty meal traditionally taken in silence that equipped them for the morning ahead. Afterwards, the teaching brothers headed straight to the classrooms to prepare materials for the day's lessons; while the lay members repaired to their appointed tasks.

Fra Celestino's first duty that day was to visit the music department. He found that the department head, Marco Villanuova, had already arrived ahead of the lessons scheduled to start at 9 a.m. The young teacher was engaged in tuning a clavichord, one of a set of period instruments they used for performing baroque music. He rose immediately from his task to greet the old brother.

"Before the boys come in," the latter said, "I wonder if you could help me carry a portrait in from the hall. The principal now wishes it to hang in the music room."

"By all means," the young man said, eagerly. "We could use something on this wall behind my desk. The dark wood paneling is a little too somber as it is and needs relief. A picture will do just fine. In fact, I was thinking of buying a small portrait of Chopin I saw in an art dealer's in Bellinzona, just for that purpose."

"Then you can save your money," Celestino said, affably. "Fra Ignacio has commissioned a portrait of the Archbishop to greet visitors as they enter the premises."

He then led the way into the main hall, drew up a small stool and stood on it to release the gilt-framed picture from its hook, Marco grasping one side to steady it. They transferred it carefully to the music room, where the lay brother nailed a bracket into the wall behind the teacher's desk. That done, they raised the heavy portrait to its new location and stepped back to admire their handiwork.

"A fine figure of a man," Marco observed, regarding a youngish individual clad in the garb of a nineteenth-century partisan. "But who, in fact, is it?" He had never consciously examined the portrait, since outside teaching staff used a side entrance and rarely entered the main hall, which led into the brothers' residential quarters.

"That," Fra Celestino announced proudly, passing a hand through his wispy white hair, "is Amadeo d'Alassio."

The music teacher eyed it with renewed interest and respect, stepping momentarily closer.

"You mean the heroic captain in Garibaldi's army during the Risorgimento?"

"The very same," Celestino averred. "He fought valiantly at the Battle of Luino, but died of his wounds—gangrene set in, I believe—after the victorious nationalists had crossed Lake Maggiore to overnight at Cannero Riviera. Amadeo is a legendary figure in the campaign for Italian unification."

"I'll be more than happy to have it in my department," Marco remarked. "How did you manage to acquire it?"

"Count Flavio offered it to us, as part payment of his son's fees."

"I didn't know that he had a son," the teacher said.

"Not surprising," Celestino said. "Emilio emigrated to New Zealand years ago, to become a sheep farmer. I understand he has done quite well for himself. Now, if you'll excuse me, I'll inform Fra Ignacio of the transfer, to make room for the Archbishop. By the way, how are rehearsals for the Pergolesi Festival going?"

"Reasonably well," Marco replied. "Some reluctance among the boys, as usual, to fill an unsympathetic female role. But apart from that everything is well according to plan."

"It will be a great evening, I have no doubt," the other said. "Offer incentives, like higher grades, and you'll soon get volunteers."

"I understand the Archbishop is attending the performance this year, for the first time. The principal won't want any hitches."

"I've never known the Festival to be anything other than first-rate," Celestino said, encouragingly. "I've always enjoyed it immensely. One of the highlights of my year, in fact."

"Very kind of you to say so," the gratified young teacher replied.

"Not at all. Some pruning to do now in the orchard, and I suppose your young charges will be arriving any minute?"

"Indeed they will," Marco Villanuova said. "Must get this vintage clavichord up to pitch before they do, for a spot of Telemann."

Telefon," the waiter announced, as George Mason was finishing his breakfast.

The detective eased his portly frame out of his window seat and crossed the hall to the phone booth with an air of expectation.

"Some news for you," Harrington said, buoyantly. "Acting on your request some days ago, we have run some checks Jill Crabtree's background. The American Embassy informed us that she was born in Boston, where she attended the Latin School. From there she went on to the University of Maine at Orono, where she read accountancy and business administration."

"That figures," Mason replied, a touch sardonically. "She's quite a creative accountant, from what I can gather. What about family background?"

"Her father's a wine importer, name of Gordon Crabtree, operating out of North Boston, the so-called Italian district."

"And the mother?"

"Of Italian descent. She was born Sophia Baldacci at Foligno, an Umbrian hill town, in 1932."

The detective recalled at once that the young American had recently met with what Alfons Goetz had described as an elderly, distinguished-looking Italian in the station buffet at Bellinzona; and that a considerable amount of money had changed hands.

"You still there?" Harrington asked, gruffly. Patience was not his most abiding quality.

"Just trying to put two and two together," Mason replied, eventually.

"Then this information could mean something to you?"

"It may, or may not, be significant," the detective said. "Too early in the day to draw firm conclusions."

"But you must surely have some useful leads, after all this time?"

"I'm working closely with Leutnant Kubler down at the Polizei Dienst. Hoping for a breakthrough fairly soon. I've also had to spend time validating my cover as a tour scout. In spare moments, I've been scouring the local bookshops in case the stolen items turn up for a quick sale."

"Without any luck so far, I take it, from your tone of voice?"

"Kubler thinks they may have left the country by now," Mason said. "But that is pure supposition, or at most an educated guess. I'm betting that they're still in Switzerland, possibly even right here in Zurich."

"I do hope your hunch is right," Harrington said. "They usually are, in my experience. Enjoy the sights, but watch you don't overstep your budget."

"I'm being as careful as I can," the detective said, hanging up the phone.

With a full morning ahead of him before his lunch appointment with Rolf Kubler, he had it in mind to check up on some of the notable sights within the city itself. His guidebook mentioned the zoo as well worth a visit, but that would involve a long tram ride up the Zurichberg, on the opposite side of the valley from Uetliberg. He decided to shelve that for a later date, thinking there were zoos and safari parks enough back home for English people to visit. He thought he could concoct some sort of cultural tour, to impress the members of St Wilfrid's at their next after-choir session at Der Waldman, that homely little *Stube* he had already grown so fond of, with its atmosphere almost of an English local pub. He sat for a few moments at a writing desk in the hotel lounge to plot an itinerary, before emerging into the bright sunlight of the mid-June day.

By eleven-thirty, he had encompassed in the course of a roughly two-mile walk the university where Albert Einstein had studied, not very far from the house that Irish author James Joyce had occupied in the thirties. Below them and closer to the city center he found the apartments overlooking a secluded garden square, where Lenin had lived in exile before heading to Russia during the Bolshevik Revolution of 1917. If he could add one or two more points of interest in this vein, he considered, he might even be able to sell the concept to a genuine tour company in

Britain. They were always on the look-out for some new and original angle to tempt the ever-swelling volume of tourists and gain the edge on competitors. Dutch bulb fields, Bavarian castles and the like were all very well; but this, he felt, was an entirely original idea that would appeal to the more sophisticated traveler. Mozart and Wagner also had connections with Zurich, as did the author of *Steppenwolf*, Hermann Hesse. He would look into it.

His wanderings led him eventually back to the Niederdorf, at the end opposite to the Hauptbahnhof. It was an area he had somehow overlooked, never having progressed along the odorous, hemmed-in alley much beyond his hotel, usually walking down to the more open Limmatquai to reach the main amenities. With over an hour to go before his meeting with Rolf Kubler, to be held at a garden restaurant even farther down the lakeside than the Wienerwald, he found a small square behind the imposing twin-spired cathedral, sat down in the shade of a pavement café, ordered coffee and lit a small cigar. According to his pocket guidebook, the Romanesque cathedral was also well worth a visit. It figured prominently in the Swiss Reformation led by Ulrich Zwingli and was now mainly notable for its magnificent organ and stained-glass windows. He would pay it a visit later.

He had not been sitting there long when, suddenly glancing across to the far side of the square, he noticed a name in quaint Gothic script above an antiquarian bookshop. His heart almost skipped a beat. BUCHHANDLUNG ANTON ZIEGLER, he read, recalling at once a most devious elderly gentleman of slight build, with a white goatee beard. As he sipped his coffee, his thoughts went back a few years to the Danube cruise he had undertaken at the behest of Chief Inspector Harrington. Intended as a rest-cure, it had turned out to be a working holiday with a vengeance,

Ziegler being one of the main players in the scramble to acquire a certain edition of *Bannerman's Guide.* He, George Mason, had bested him and exposed a former Nazi spy working in a senior position in Whitehall. The case had earned him a special commendation from the Superintendant of Police.

George Mason chuckled to himself. What a turn-up this was, and why had he not recalled before now that Anton Ziegler owned a bookshop near the Niederdorf? The Swiss had volunteered that nugget himself during the cruise. Perhaps it was because the details of that eventful voyage, so vivid at the time, had receded in his memory with the passage of time. Yet it was one more plausible link to far-right European politics. He was of a mind to cross the square and visit the bookshop, just to ascertain if any of the missing books had turned up there. It was at least worth a try. But would Ziegler recognize him and would it put him in some way on his guard? It seemed unlikely, but it was a chance the detective felt he had to take. This was too good an opportunity to pass up. He drained his cup, extinguished the butt of his cigar, settled his account and strolled across the square.

On reaching the bookshop, he paused momentarily outside to examine the window display. It consisted mainly of art books and medieval maps, tastefully arranged. In the doorway, as he approached, were printed notices, among which he instantly recognized one advertising the Pergolesi Festival Margaret Fern had urged him to attend. He noted the date and entered the premises, to be greeted by a series of linking small rooms, much like a warren, extending well back into the building. It would take several days, he mused, to examine all the items on the cluttered shelves, which at least seemed clearly marked as to contents.

"*Guten Tag*," came a voice from behind the counter, as its owner, a balding gentleman with wire-rimmed spectacles, glanced up from an open catalog. "Can I be of some assistance?"

"Just browsing, thanks," the detective said, stepping into an adjoining room to look for books on architecture, specifically for a copy of Palladio's *Architettura* in the original Italian. By alphabetical arrangement, he found several works by that author, including what seemed a rare early French translation of his famous treatise, but nothing in Italian. Nor, as he progressed to the Histories section farther back in the musty, almost claustrophobic depths of the shop, did he come across any editions of Ackerman's *History of Westminster Abbey*. Modern fiction occupied a larger, more open area towards the front of the building and, while it contained several first-edition Hemingways in pristine dust jackets, there was only a reprint edition of *The Old Man and the Sea*. He felt a frisson of disappointment as he returned to the Architecture section and took down the French edition of the Palladio that had earlier caught his eye. Opening it carefully, he marveled at the illustrative plates, the quality of the paper and the elegant binding, while disregarding the French text, which he did not understand. The price, at 20,000 euros, did not surprise him in the least, and he could understand the appeal of collecting such beautifully-wrought objects.

"Visiting Zurich?" the individual behind the counter enquired, amicably.

"In a manner of speaking," George Mason replied.

"And you collect rare books?"

"I have a professional interest in them," he said, guardedly.

"Any particular field?"

The detective shook his head, unwilling to be drawn into a protracted discussion.

"We have the most comprehensive collection of antiquarian items and first-edition novels in Zurich."

"I can well believe that," Mason said, genuinely impressed.

As he spoke, he caught the sound of a door closing softly somewhere near at hand. He glanced questioningly towards the other man.

"The proprietor, Herr Ziegler, is stocktaking this week and wishes on no account to be disturbed. Otherwise, I would gladly have introduced you to him. He is far more knowledgable than I."

"Herr…?" the detective enquired.

"Leverkov," returned the other, promptly. "Oleg Leverkov, at your service. I am Anton Ziegler's assistant. If you should by any chance have an interest in old Cyrillic manuscripts, that is my special field."

"Russian is not my strong suit, I'm afraid," Mason said. "I barely get by with German and French, as it is."

"There is a strong market in Zurich for old Russian collectibles," Leverkov explained, expansively. "My brother-in-law deals in medieval icons and recordings of Orthodox liturgical music from his store on the Munsterplatz. He is enjoying a very profitable season so far."

"American customers mainly, I expect?"

"But not exclusively. Many Russian émigrés fled to the United States during the Bolshevik Revolution, as they did to Western Europe. Their descendants are often on the look-out for memorabilia, for sentimental as much as any other reason."

"You yourself, I take it, are of Russian origin?"

Oleg Leverkov nodded curtly.

"My parents defected to the West just after the war," he volunteered. "They were members of a music ensemble embarking on a European tour. They sought asylum in Stockholm as soon as their ship, the *Baltika*, docked there."

"Most interesting," George Mason said, sensing that he was in for a full biography if he lingered. Stepping towards the door, he said: "I'll call again soon."

"*Auf wiedersehen*," the other said, amiably.

The minute George Mason stepped outside, Anton Ziegler emerged from the stockroom to confront his assistant.

"I was chatting with a tourist from England," Leverkov remarked half apologetically, since the encounter had interrupted his cataloging. "An amateur, I would say, rather than a serious collector."

"I recognized the voice at once from the stockroom," the proprietor said, ominously. "If the person who has just left is your typical English tourist, then I'm a reincarnation of William Tell."

"He spent most of the time in the Architecture and History collections," the assistant explained, "showing particular interest in our early French edition of Palladio. Took it down and examined it most thoroughly. I thought at one point he was going to buy it."

"On a policeman's salary?" Ziegler scoffed.

"*Bitte?*" Oleg Leverkov said, not quite able to believe his ears.

"That was Inspector George Mason, Scotland Yard Special Branch. I crossed swords with him, in a manner of speaking, a few years back on a Danube cruise. I'd know him anywhere, even though I got only the briefest glance. Lucky for us that we moved the key items on at the weekend."

"You mean he's on the track of the first editions?"

"What else?" Ziegler replied. "I'd stake my entire stock that that's exactly what he's after."

"But why would he come in here, unless he's been tipped off?"

"Our security's cast-iron," the other said, more collectedly. "I expect he was just fishing. Doing the rounds of the second-hand bookshops, as a matter of routine. I doubt he will return, having drawn a blank. George Mason doesn't waste his time."

⌁

On leaving the bookshop, George Mason took a right turn by the cathedral and descended the steep, cobbled street to the river embankment. From there, he covered the short distance to the busy tram intersection at Belle Vue, crossed over at the pedestrian signal and continued along the strand. The Wienerwald was doing a brisk lunch-hour trade at its fully-occupied pavement tables. Beyond it, gaps in the lakeside buildings grew wider, to allow large areas of manicured lawn shaded by overhanging trees. It was a favorite spot for university students to bring their picnics or sunbathe in the free hours between lectures; for young women to perform aerobics, and for the occasional tramp to collect discarded cigarette ends or beg money for a drink. All of life was there. The lake itself was slowly filling with sail for what promised to be a breezy afternoon. The ferry to distant Rapperswil sounded its horn.

Mason's objective lay well beyond the Wienerwald and the luxury hotels, like the Bauer au Lac, neighboring it. By his estimation, it must be at least a mile from Belle Vue, as part of Rolf Kubler's scheme to introduce him to the city's scenic attractions. He was certainly enjoying the walk in bracing fresh air that would sharpen his appetite for lunch, musing as he went on his recent visit to Ziegler's bookshop. Had the proprietor intentionally kept out of sight to avoid an encounter, since he had almost certainly overheard him speaking with Leverkov before shutting the stockroom door tight? Had he recognized his voice, Mason wondered, eventually deciding that it was unlikely after the passage of time. Had Ziegler something to hide? That was the interesting question, in view of the Swiss's past involvement with an extreme right-wing organization that sought to protect former Nazis. A return visit to the Niederdorf premises might well yield results, unless Anton Ziegler was now decidedly on his guard.

Leutnant Kubler was already seated at table in the garden restaurant abutting Lake Zurich at the point where it broadened considerably from its narrower city confines and gave panoramic views of the snow-capped alps, which seemed somehow much closer and more defined against the azure sky. The detective eased his way carefully down the short flight of stone steps between the colorful floral displays, to join his Swiss colleague at the far side of the restaurant where a wooden deck overhung the choppy water, giving patrons the illusion almost of being afloat.

"They do a very good pizza," Kubler said, as his English colleague sat down rather heavily. "I propose that we share one, since they're rather large, with a side salad."

"You certainly pick some interesting spots," George Mason said, with approval.

"This little place is a favorite of mine, well away from the bustle of the city. I thought you might appreciate it, too. Now what will it be, the pepperoni or the ham?"

Mason glanced briefly at the menu card and laid it aside.

"Pizza will do just fine," he replied. "Let's take the ham, with artichokes and olives as extras. And a demi-carafe of red wine."

"They have an excellent German red, from the Ahr Valley," the Swiss suggested.

"I'll give it a go," Mason responded, associating Germany only with white wines, with Rieslings, hocks and the like.

"You're in for a pleasant surprise," Kubler said, conspiratorially.

He placed the order with the waiter and sat back to take in the view across the water.

"There's been an interesting development," he remarked, eventually.

"Oh?" enquired Mason, sitting bolt upright.

"An arrest in Schaffhausen on Tuesday, at the polytechnic," the Swiss explained. "A student by the name of Erik Muntener was caught in the act of removing a valuable reference work from the technical library. Kaporal Goetz has been questioning him."

"With what result?" Mason demanded at once.

"Muntener claims it was a first offense, to help finance a drug addiction, and that he was acting alone."

"Then how did he plan to dispose of the goods?" Mason enquired, dubiously.

"On the Internet, apparently," Kubler replied, gauging the other's reaction. "No questions asked. Just a straightforward sale. It happens all the time."

Refreshment arrived at that point, commandeering their attention. Mason sampled the unusual German red and found its mellow, honeyed palate to his liking. They split the pizza and the bowl of endive-and-tomato salad, fending off the sparrows that soon descended on their table from the nearby sycamores. Pizza was best eaten warm, in the Englishman's view. Business could wait.

"I see you always have good appetite," Kubler said approvingly, the moment his companion nudged the finished plate aside.

"It's the legwork that comes with the job," Mason replied, a trifle self-consciously, in case the Swiss was really referring to his waistline. "The lakeside air also piques the palate."

"I like a man who enjoys his food. How about dessert and coffee?"

"I'll have a coffee, but skip the dessert," Mason said. "I've been thinking that it's time we brought the tax people in again."

"Another special audit?" the lieutenant asked, in surprise.

"At the premises of Manfred Bott AG, in Bern."

"I don't quite follow," the other said, with a baffled look.

"I have it on good authority—from the horse's mouth, as we say in England—that my fellow bass in St Wilfrid's choir, Mr Max Fifield, was in Schaffhausen that very day on a sales assignment for Manfred Bott AG."

"And you think he may have some connection with the arrested student?"

"I'm thinking there is at least a possibility," George Mason declared, "that Max Fifield is Erik Muntener's contact. It's certainly worth looking into."

"How do you propose the tax investigators can help?" Kubler asked, skeptically.

"You yourself told me that a special audit can take place at any time, at any business premises, without arousing the least suspicion. If the tax people visit Manfred Bott's, they could among other matters examine the recent sales records for all their representatives. We could get a complete print-out of Fifield's activities over the last few months and see if we can tie his field trips in with the sites of the stolen books."

"A brilliant idea," the Swiss lieutenant commented, with an appreciative glance at his colleague.

"There's something else you could help me with," Mason then said.

"By all means," Kubler replied, at once. "Just name it, we'll do our best."

The detective slowly drained his coffee, glanced wistfully at the strawberry cheesecake on the dessert menu without ordering it, and said:

"Chief Inspector Harrington back at Scotland Yard has come up with some information on Jill Crabtree's background. Her mother, Sophia Baldacci, was apparently born near the Umbrian town of Foligno. It might be useful if you could get the Italian police to report on any questionable activities in that area and report back to you."

"So that we can try to nail the source of the funds Jill Crabtree obtained from the elderly Italian gentleman at Bellinzona?" Kubler asked,

"It's a long shot, I know," Mason said. "But it's all we have to go off for the present."

"I'll contact the Carabinieri straight away, soon as I get back to my office," the other promised, rising to walk to his parked car while George Mason lingered over a refill of coffee and lit one of his small Dutch cigars. He would turn over the latest developments in his mind and enjoy the remainder of the afternoon by the lake, before returning to his hotel.

chapter 8

MAX FIFIELD SAT at a window seat in the *Schnellzug* to Zurich, taking in the unfolding scenery of the Bernese Oberland, while skimming through a copy of the London *Times*. He had just filed his sales returns at the head office of his employer, Manfred Bott AG, and was looking forward to a relaxed weekend and a spot of sailing with Hugh Selby on the Zugersee. It had been one of his more successful weeks, clouded only by the failure of Erik Muntener to make their assignment at Schaffhausen. The more he reflected on that, the more likely it seemed that the student had been delayed, perhaps by a tutorial or by technical problems in the computer department. There was no way of knowing at this precise moment. He would have to wait until Muntener contacted him, hopefully very soon. He was also wondering why Anton Ziegler had requested an urgent meeting that very afternoon, telephoning him at his Bern office in a voice, not so much of alarm, as of genuine concern. The shrewd book dealer usually had things well under his control, being the most phlegmatic of men. He would soon find out what, if anything, was eating him, as the express train picked up speed beyond Olten.

Finishing the report on the First Test Match between England and India at the Oval—England had a slight first-innings lead, thanks to a century by David Gower—he checked the newspaper for any relevant political comment, found none and laid it aside. He had bought it mainly for the cricket, a passion dating from his schooldays, when he had opened the batting with some distinction for the senior team. His thoughts turned to St Wilfrid's choir and in particular to Jill Crabtree. He had known her for over two years now, even more closely during the last six months, since she had begun inviting him back to her apartment following their customary visit to Der Waldman after choir. Since they lived in the same general direction, it had seemed almost a logical step, one that he had not in any way resisted. He sensed, increasingly of late, that she was expecting things to move a significant stage further and he was wondering how best to extricate himself from a committed relationship. He valued his bachelor freedom too much to entertain thoughts of marriage and all that that implied. He led a full life in Zurich, conscious always of the possibility that the Britannia Party would recall him to England ahead of the next general election. His best tactic with Jill, he felt, was to leave matters just as they were. She was a smart and independent woman who would draw her own conclusions soon enough and move on, while remaining good friends.

The city was full of eligible bachelors, he reflected, as the southern limits of Lake Zurich suddenly appeared beyond the carriage window, indicating that he would reach his destination in about thirty minutes. There were several unattached males on the staff of her school, for example, as well as eligible parish members unconnected with the choir. And there was that chap Marco she had mentioned from San Isidoro's, whom she had invited to the Kantorei concert and the next carol service. There was almost a family relationship there already, he felt, considering Marco's friendship with Count Flavio and the latter's closeness to Jill's mother. As they sped through Kilchberg, one of the city's wealthier suburbs, he gathered together his few effects and moved further down the train, to effect a quicker exit.

Having reached the station concourse, he moved swiftly to the end platform and caught the funicular to Uetliberg. A brisk walk from the hilltop terminus brought him to Der Waldhaus, where Anton Ziegler was sitting unperturbed outside, nursing a stein of export beer.

"Glad you could make it so readily," he remarked, by way of greeting, as the book salesman sat down.

"You caught me just as I was completing my sales returns," Max Fifield said. "I was on the point of leaving the office."

"Did you bring the material from Schaffhausen?" Ziegler enquired, expectantly.

Max's face fell. He was hoping the antiquarian would not refer to it so soon.

"Erik Muntener failed to appear," he replied, matter-of-factly. "May have been delayed, or possibly even ill. I couldn't hang about all day. Had a sales appointment shortly after lunch."

"No great concern," the other said. "There's still time."

"You didn't bring me up here, surely, to discuss Erik Muntener?" Max challenged.

Anton Ziegler quaffed his beer thoughtfully.

"What will *you* have?" he offered.

"Same as yours," the other replied, as the attractive, dirndl-clad waitress hovered near their table.

"There's been a rather curious development," Ziegler said, at length.

"How curious?"

"An Englishman called George Mason entered my shop mid-week. My assistant Oleg Leverkov claims he showed great interest in our French edition of Palladio and in first editions of Ernest Hemingway."

Max Fifield gave him a rather startled look.

"A fiftyish, rather portly chap?" he enquired.

The antiquarian nodded.

"I know him!" Max exclaimed. "He quite recently joined our church choir, as a second bass. Quite a decent voice, too. He's a tour scout for a travel firm in the north of England, but I'm surprised he's interested in old books. Doesn't seem to fit his image at all."

"He has a very keen interest in them, I assure you," Ziegler said.

"Come to think of it," Max recalled, "he did attend the book fair at Rutli Meadow."

"With what object in mind?"

"He was on the look-out for classic travel guides," Max explained. "The kind with black-and-white photographic plates. Or so he claimed."

"Would it surprise you to know that, far from being a tour scout, he is in fact Inspector George Mason of Scotland Yard Special Branch?"

Max Fifield sat back and gasped aloud.

"How on earth would you know that?" he said, with a feeling that all along, ever since the day Mason had joined the choir, he had felt there was some sort of mystery about him. Jill Crabtree and Hugh Selby had felt the same way.

"I had dealings with him a few years ago, on a Danube cruise," the other said.

"So we're now to consider ourselves under investigation?" the non-plussed salesman remarked, slowly digesting the import of Ziegler's remarks.

"He won't find anything," Ziegler said, confidently. "The material's already moved on to a safe house he'll never latch onto in a hundred years. And soon enough, it'll move out of the country altogether."

"That's a relief," Max said, taking a long swig at his freshly-drawn ale.

"But perhaps it would be better if you suspended your activities in that area for the time being," the older man proposed. "We cannot afford any slip-ups at this juncture."

"I'll contact Erik," the salesman said, a touch uneasily, "and tell him to restore the stolen property to Schaffhausen Polytechnic. Scotland Yard Special Branch, eh? However did they become involved?"

Anton Ziegler gave a rather enigmatic smile.

"Heaven only knows that," he replied. "All I do know is that it would be a very serious mistake to underestimate Mr Mason."

"We'll have to lie low," Max considered. "Hopefully he'll find nothing and then move on."

"Don't count on it," Ziegler said, ominously. "Now, since you won't yet have eaten, what will you have?"

Max Fifield took up the menu and studied it briefly, unsure if he had any real appetite. Mainly to humor the older man, he said:

"Why don't we share a Walliserteller and have another beer?"

"Cold cuts is fine by me," Ziegler replied, "if you're sure that's all you want."

Around noon that same day, George Mason found himself half-way along the Bahnhofstrasse, one of Europe's most elegant streets, with its fashion boutiques, art galleries, jewelers and gourmet restaurants. Trams plied smoothly between the Hauptbahnhof and the lake, well-dressed pedestrians filled the sidewalks and the open-air cafes beneath the chestnut trees did a brisk trade. Seeking an indoor venue to get a break from the heat, he mounted the stairs of a Victorian building on his right, to reach a second-floor establishment named Kretzler's, which advertised home-baked quiche and Danish pastries.

Once inside and comfortably ensconced at a window table, he ordered a pot of coffee and withdrew from his jacket pocket the fax that Alfons Goetz had sent to his hotel that morning, just as he was finishing breakfast. It outlined the results of his inquiry into the academic background of Laszlo Polke, whom the director of Succor had alerted to the police. The detective read it with keen interest. It seemed that the young man had been a prominent member of the right-wing Edel Student Corps, one of the type that wore military regalia and engaged in duelling with swords, often sporting small facial scars in testimony. The police corporal stressed that these activities and rituals were in no sense neo-Nazi, being more a continuation of a tradition dating from the Middle Ages. According to the fax, and George Mason was grateful for the detailed explanation, the student corps originated when the first universities were founded, as far back as the twelfth century. A higher education then was the prerogative of sons of the aristocracy, who often had to travel long distances on foot or on horse, carrying large purses of money for tuition and lodging. They wore swords to protect themselves from highway robbers, often traveling in small groups for mutual protection. In more modern times, they operated much like student fraternities across the globe, the older members helping the new arrivals settle in and generally looking out for their welfare. Hence corps membership, while remaining open to all-comers, tended in practice to be drawn from a particular region of Germany, such as Saxony or Westphalia.

He refolded the instructive document, replaced it in his pocket and poured coffee from an elegant china jug with floral motifs into a matching cup. What Alfons Goetz had come up with was most interesting. He felt he was beginning to see a sort of pattern in this curious sequence of events, a pattern of decidedly right-wing political sympathies. Max Fifield, Nazi sympathizer Anton Ziegler, and now this Laszlo Polke, whom he had not so far met, all leaned the same way. Were they involved in some kind of plot, his suspicious mind wondered? And were they acting individually, or in collusion?

He was about to take his first sip when he espied Margaret Fern dressed in a yellow two-piece suit approaching his table, with a broad smile of recognition.

"Imagine meeting you here, George," she said, cheerily. "May I join you?"

"Please do," he said, indicating the vacant chair opposite.

"Still taking in the tourist sights?" she enquired, sitting down and immediately scanning the menu.

"In a manner of speaking," Mason replied, evasively. "What about you?"

"I've managed to get an extended lunch-hour," she explained, quickly ordering a prawn salad with an orange juice.

"It's a very warm day," the detective said, requesting a grilled ham sandwich while the waitress was at hand. "Thought I'd be cooler indoors for a while."

"Can't stay too long," Margaret explained. "Doing a bit of shopping for a wedding present. A colleague of mine is getting married tomorrow and, as usual, I've left things rather late."

"A fellow-worker at Succor?"

The young woman nodded.

"And how are things going at your organization?"

Margaret's face clouded slightly.

"Very well, in the main. But there have been unaccountable delays in one of our key projects, a hostel for young women at Debrecen."

"What sort of delays?" Mason enquired, keenly interested.

"You wouldn't really understand," she replied, rather brusquely.

"I suppose not," he said untruthfully, thinking of Laszlo Polke.

"Are you enjoying singing in the choir?" she asked, abruptly changing the subject.

"Very much so," he replied. "I especially like the Vaughan Williams."

"Max is so pleased to have you," she went on, "to strengthen the bass section."

George Mason felt gratified at that remark; it could only mean that his cover was fully intact.

Their refreshment arrived, occupying her full attention. She was evidently in a hurry to eat and go shopping. Mason observed her quietly, between mouthfuls of his grilled panini sandwich. She looked very smart, he thought, in her cotton two-piece, with her dark hair newly permed, no doubt for the wedding tomorrow. He would have liked to ask her about her colleague Laszlo Polke, whom she knew much better than he did, but he could not risk at this stage arousing any suspicions about his presence in Zurich.

"Don't forget," she said, as she was finishing her drink and preparing to leave, "to look up the Pergolesi Festival. I feel sure your clients would enjoy it. The venue alone is quite spectacular."

"In the southern alps?" he enquired, only vaguely interested.

"Between Locarno and Bellinzona."

Promising to meet him at St Wilfrid's on Sunday, she settled her bill and hastily left, leaving him to finish his snack in solitude. He took out Kaporal Goetz's fax and re-read it, deciding on the strength of it to do some further research.

Zentral Bibliothek, the main library, was a fair walk in the midday heat from Kretzler's, being situated close to the university. Mason entered the cool, air-conditioned interior with relief and strode up to the Enquiry Desk for assistance. The duty clerk directed him to the shelves housing books on politics and sociology, where he eventually found what he was looking for. It was a recently-published volume on political movements in East Europe, written by a professor from the former East Germany. The chapter on Hungary included short accounts of two right-wing organizations. With the aid of a hefty English-German dictionary from the Languages section, the detective worked laboriously through the text until he had satisfied himself that Zeged's aims and manifesto most closely approximated to what he had divined of Laszlo Polke's own sympathies. Zeged had links to similar organizations in other members of the former Soviet bloc, most notably Poland; but all shared the same nationalist views and were concerned to prevent their respective countries from joining the European Union.

Like many Britishers, George Mason had mixed views himself on that subject. He liked the concept of a Common Market, with free exchange of goods, peoples and ideas. But he thought it should not go much beyond a free-trade area and was strongly against the push towards a federal state. It pleased him that Britain had kept its own currency and could decide its own fiscal policies; but he was unhappy as a police officer that the European Court of Justice could override British legal decisions. England, after all, had introduced trial by jury in open courts, or assizes, as far back as the twelfth century, during the reign of Henry 11, the first Plantagenet, a system much expanded by his son King John, of Magna Carta fame. In continental Europe, by contrast, people were secretly denounced to the authorities, tortured until they confessed, and convicted without even knowing who their accuser was. We needed no lessons from across the English Channel, George Mason felt, on how to administer justice. And if European integration meant that there could be no more wars of the type that had periodically ravaged the continent over the last several centuries, whether for dynastic, religious or ideological reasons, it was commendable on that score alone. As he replaced his reference material and strolled towards the exit and out into the bright sunlight, he allowed himself a degree of sympathy with the views of individuals like Max Fifield or Lazslo Polke; but only up to a point and always with the proviso that, as a public servant, his personal views on such matters were irrelevant.

He began to wonder, as he strolled back down Ramistrasse towards his hotel, into what murky waters his enquiries were likely to lead him. He had not had much experience of political movements, except to cast his vote from time to time as a dutiful citizen and generally opting for middle-of-the-road policies as opposed to either the far-right or the far-left, both extremes being foreign to him. His English temperament favored the middle way in most areas of life and valued the art of compromise. What, he wondered, was the real significance of the stolen books, the embezzlement and the mysterious sums of money originating in Italy? It was all very puzzling, yet at the same time highly intriguing and challenging. He had to admit to himself that, as Chief

Inspector Harrington had often reminded him, he enjoyed nothing more than a battle of wits. If the likes of Anton Ziegler were involved, he would be well-assured of that.

chapter 9

Count Flavio de Montesedina finished a light lunch of prosciutto ham and olives with freshly-baked bread rolls and a glass of chilled Soave on the terrace of his villa overlooking Lake Maggiore. His wife Amelia had not joined him on this occasion, choosing to remain at her studio since midmorning to put the finishing touches to some paintings she was preparing for the Milan Bienniale the following week. Rising from his wicker chair, the elderly aristocrat crossed the patio and made a brief inspection of his flower beds, dead-heading roses and adjusting some straggling sweet peas on their climbing frame, before repairing to his room to pack an overnight bag. Half an hour later, he bade goodbye to his cook-housekeeper, Signora Giacinta, indicating that he would be returning late Sunday evening, and made his way down to the strand for the twenty-minute walk to the jetty to catch the Friday afternoon ferry to Locarno.

He was in good time to watch the large, stately vessel approach from the south, half filled with passengers who had boarded at Arona. He joined the short queue at the Stresa booking-office, bought his ticket and waited for the boat to dock before ascending the gangway to find a vacant seat on the forward open deck. When he had the time, he generally chose this mode of travel north into Switzerland, preferring the fresh lake air to the confines of a crowded railway compartment. He listened with satisfaction as the boat's powerful engines revved, moving it clear of the short wooden jetty and out into open water, past the aptly-named Isola Bella and the smaller island close to it once owned by the famous conductor, Arturo Toscanini, and used as a getaway from the demands of the concert circuit.

In another hour or so, the boat would call at Cannero, from where it was only a short voyage to Locarno. He would then take the Locarno-Bellinzona mail train, which would slowly but surely, stopping at every village station, bring him to his intermediate destination and an early dinner with Marco Villanuova at a restaurant in Bellinzona Later on, he would continue his journey by rail on the short final leg to Lugano. The prospect pleased him considerably, as the vessel left the scenic islands in its wake and the Swiss Alps, hung with cumulus, came into sharper relief. At long last, after months of solo work and fund-raising, he was about to meet the other members of the inner circle, so far known only to *Il Direttore,* who had insisted on rigid compartmentalization of their respective functions. Now that the time was drawing nearer to a realisation of their well-laid plans, he was much intrigued as to who these individuals might be, feeling assured that they would be at least as prominent in their own fields as he was. *Il Direttore*, summoned at the last minute to a conference in Geneva that he could not avoid, had in fact offered him the chair of what was scheduled, barring unforeseen circumstances, to be their penultimate meeting. He would concentrate on establishing a good rapport among the members of the circle, and on ironing out any key differences of opinion or views on tactics that might arise.

The young music master from Collegio San Isidoro was waiting to greet him as the stopping train from Locarno pulled slowly into Bellinzona at 5.35 p.m. He carried under his arm a violin he had had reconditioned in the city that afternoon, to loan to a first-year student who wished to join the school orchestra.

"*Buona sera*," he greeted warmly, as the count stepped out onto the platform clutching his overnight bag and looking a little weary from his trip.

"A fine evening it is, too," Flavio responded, grasping Marco's free hand in a firm shake.

The younger man led the way out of the station and along a sloping, tree-lined street bustling with evening commuter traffic. They walked for about ten minutes before pausing to weigh up the menu posted outside Rosario's, an intimate restaurant with lace curtains and colorful window boxes, mainly of nasturtiums and petunias..

"I booked a table for six o'clock," Marco said, consulting his watch.

"Can't say I know this place," Flavio replied, rather doubtfully.

"Fra Celestino recommended it to me personally. The owner is married to his niece."

"Then it must be good," observed the count as they stepped inside, to be greeted by the warm glow from the pizza oven.

The dapper waiter led them to a corner table covered by a red checkered cloth and decorated with a small vase of flowers, presenting them with an elaborate menu as they sat down.

"I'll have the salmon trout, with linguini and asparagus," Flavio decided after a few moments' deliberation, thinking the fish was probably caught locally.

"I'll try the octopus," Marco said, adventurously, "with wild rice and mushrooms."

"Let's split a half-carafe of Valpolicella," the other suggested. "to help it down."

"Fine by me," Marco agreed, as the waiter approached.

"Now tell me, young man, how things are going at the college?"

"Preparations are well under way for the Festival," Marco replied. "I expect it to be one of the best productions we've ever staged during my tenure as music director. You and Amelia will be coming, won't you?"

Count Flavio averted his gaze, to a large print of Lake Como on the opposite wall.

"It depends very much on circumstances," he replied, non-committally. "I take it we shall be able to obtain tickets at a later date, if we so decide?"

"I'll hold two back for you in reserve," the younger man said. "I can always dispose of them nearer the time if you are prevented from attending."

"That's very kind of you," the count remarked, as they both applied themselves to the gourmet cuisine, served with much aplomb by the waiter.

"By the way," the count continued, when they were half-way through, "how did you get on with my young acquaintance, Jill Crabtree?"

"Excellently," Marco replied. "She was very impressed with San Isidoro and invited me to some concerts at Zurigo, later this year."

Count Flavio gave a knowing smile, as he raised a glass of his favorite light red wine to his lips.

"She's on the look-out for a husband," he teased.

"What on earth makes you say that?" the other replied, studiously carving his octopus and affecting disinterest.

"Sophia, her mother, informed me in one of her letters. Jill wants to settle permanently in Switzerland, but she can only do that if she marries a Swiss."

"Thanks for the warning," Marco said, intrigued. "I'll be on my guard."

"You could do much worse," Flavio proposed. "An attractive young woman, musical, of good family and half-Italian. Father successful in business. What more could you want?"

The music master was at that point more concerned with coping with his unusual dish than with romantic scenarios. He ate in silence for a while and refilled his wine glass. Count Flavio, satisfied that he had sown the idea in the young man's mind, resolved not to touch on the subject again. He could at least report back to Sophia that he had effected a useful, if not a promising, introduction.

"You brought the music with you?" he asked expectantly, as they both sat back to finish their wine.

Marco Villnuova reached inside his briefcase, drew out a small sheaf of photocopies and placed them ceremoniously on the table.

"Six copies of *Nessun Dorma*," he announced, "in my own choral arrangement."

"Excellent," the count remarked, appreciatively scanning the music before placing it safely in the side pouch of his overnight bag. "*Grazie* for all the hard work you've put in."

"I'd gladly come down to Lugano with you, to conduct it in person," the younger man said, optimistically.

"I'm afraid, my dear Marco," Flavio replied, with genuine regret, "that would be quite impossible. The meeting is highly confidential. Not even I know who else will be present."

The music master eyed him closely for a few moments, wondering what exactly it was that his good friend was into, concluding ruefully that it was also the reason for his inability to commit himself and Amelia to attending his opera production. The Italian couple had never before, to his almost certain knowledge, passed up a Pergolesi Festival.

On impulse, he said: "Will Jill Crabtree be in attendance?"

"Whatever makes you say that?" the astonished count replied.

"I was wondering if that large sum of money you handed to her a while back had some bearing on Lugano."

Flavio eyed him sternly.

"My dear friend," he said, "do not get involved in matters that don't concern you. You have played your part admirably so far. What transpired between me and the young American was an arrangement of a purely private nature."

"I did not mean to intrude," Marco apologized, sensing now that his surmisings were way off mark.

Count Flavio toyed with his wine glass, while thinking up some plausible explanation to satisfy the younger man's misplaced curiosity once and for all.

"Jill intends to buy a small property in one of Zurich's nicer suburbs," he prevaricated, in a softer tone. "Needs a bit of help with the deposit, that's all. Couldn't hand her a check because her bank account is temporarily frozen, owing to some little financial difficulty she had recently. I promised her mother I would assist."

"Very noble of you," Marco observed appreciatively, as they called the waiter over to settle their bill before they parted on their customary good terms and went their separate ways, to the parking lot and the railway station respectively.

General Guido Granelli packed his overnight bag and left his home around mid-afternoon that same day. His wife Silvia drove him in their Alfa Romeo to Milano Centrale, where he boarded the William Tell Express on its return journey to Zurich. Occupying a seat in the first-class section of the train, he took out his half-read copy of *La Stampa* and perused a long article on the environment which focused mainly on the rising temperature of the Mediterranean Sea, the growing pollution and the steady increase of invasive species. It was a subject close to his heart, since his family had for several generations owned a small island off the Ligurian coast, where he felt his bathing and fishing interests increasingly threatened. It was time, he considered, that the government took firm action and tackled the root of the problem, which to his mind lay mainly in industrial effluents.

Now in his mid-fifties, the general was a career soldier who, unlike many of his fellow senior officers, had not come up through the ranks. He owed his relatively swift string of promotions in part to family connections, in part to his natural abilities and aptitude for the job. His career had been successful up to a point, in that he had taken part in several UN peace-keeping missions to the world's trouble spots, receiving for his efforts numerous decorations and commendations. He was now commanding officer of the 5th Light Infantry, with overall responsibility for homeland defense. Silvia and he, however, had fully expected that he would have progressed by now to a prestige post in the NATO High Command. His wife still held out hopes of that, being in some ways more ambitious than he was; but Guido realized only too well that he had been by-passed in favor of a younger officer who had spent his entire service to date in military planning and logistics. Given the international character of NATO, it did not seem likely that they would appoint another Italian to a senior post before his mandatory retirement at the age of sixty.

The William Tell Express soon left behind the sprawling Milan connurbation to speed along the right flank of Lake Maggiore, making its first stop at Luino. From his window seat, General Guido got a good view of the busy little town, where stalls were being erected ahead of the outdoor weekend market that drew buyers and vendors from a wide hinterland and from such communities as Cannero and Cannobio just across the lake. He refolded his newspaper, purchased a small bottle of Perrier from the passing trolley and mused on the weekend's likely course of events, as the *Schnellzug* quit the lakeside town and headed non-stop to Bellinzona. Uppermost in his mind was the composition of the inner circle—*il cuore*, as he preferred to think of it—that so far was known only to *Il Direttore*. Their competence, dedication and secrecy were crucial to the success of their enterprise and he was counting on them to have made their respective preparations as carefully as he had. With civilians one could never really tell; they lacked the discipline of the military mind and were often sloppy over minor details.

When the train duly arrived at Bellinzona in the early evening, he crossed the platfrom and stood waiting for his connection to Lugano, paying no heed to a silver-haired Italian-looking gentleman standing twenty paces to his left and toting an overnight bag very similar to his own. The Lugano train, originating in Bern, eased into the station on time and he was soon on his way to the lakeside city, to his discerning mind one of the jewels of Ticino. On arrival, he caught a cab, giving curt directions to the Hotel Papavero, marveling as they drove at how the mountains seemed to rise straight out of the water on the opposite bank, conveying a rather hemmed-in atmosphere very different from the more open vistas along Lake Maggiore. It was a little after eight by the time he checked in at Reception, collected his key and mounted the stairs to his second-floor room. He phoned Silvia to assure her of his safe arrival, before taking a quick shower, re-dressing and helping himself to a scotch-and-soda from the room mini-bar. Relaxing into a deep armchair, he switched on the television for the mid-evening news and its usual catalog, in his view, of government waste and incompetence.

It was just turned nine o'clock when he made his way down to the first-floor Function Room, following the instructions he had received shortly before leaving Milan. He found, as he had anticipated, just a handful of people mingling informally near a table of tasteful hors d'oeuvres and several opened bottles of *Fiore di Foligno,* one of his favorite white wines. A silver-haired gentleman, whom he vaguely recognized, approached him at once.

"Count Flavio de Montesedina," his greeter said, by way of introduction. "You must be…"

"General Guido Granelli," returned the military man, dressed in a plain gray suit.

"Delighted to make your acquaintance," the count assured him. "No doubt you are a little peckish after your trip from…?"

"Milano," replied the general, firmly shaking hands and scanning the buffet with keen interest. "Now what do we have here?"

"Smoked salmon, prawns, vol-au-vents, et cetera. An attractive spread, but first let me pour you a glass of my estate wine I had shipped in specially for the occasion. Then I'll introduce you to the other members of our privileged little circle."

The military man accepted the proffered drink and commenced serving himself from the buffet, as Count Flavio gently interrupted conversations in progress.

118

"Ladies and gentlemen," he announced. "Now that we are all present, and none of us has previously met, I propose that we introduce ourselves individually and briefly indicate our respective roles. I am Count Flavio de Montesedina, the chair for tomorrow's meeting in the absence of *Il Direttore,* who has been called to a conference in Geneva. And on my left…?"

"Anton Ziegler," spoke an elderly man with a wispy goatee beard. "Antiquarian book dealer from Zurich, in charge of fund-raising activities."

"Professore Ilona Rosso," said his neighbor, a well-built, middle-aged woman clad in a dark two-piece suit. "I head the faculty of political theory at Instituto Reale di San Remo. My brief is constitutional implications and related matters."

A murmur of appreciation spread through the small gathering, as the professor glanced towards her immediate neighbor, a short, balding gentleman sporting a flamboyant bow tie.

"Alessandro Pignatelli," that person said. "President of the Association of Small Businesses. I operate a large printing company near Torino and have charge of publicity and media relationships."

"Giulietta Ferrara," the second woman said. She was the youngest person in the room, an attractive brunette clad in a close-fitting beige dress, with careful make-up and large, pendant ear-rings. "I am an electronics expert responsible for security. I have already checked this venue for bugging devices and shall complete sound-proofing procedures before tomorrow's conference. After that, I shall have no further duties."

Count Flavio turned to the last-remaining member of the group, who had been quietly enjoying the gourmet buffet in the background and sipping Montesedina Estate wine, seemingly not over-impressed with the brief biographies. Aware of his own key role, he laid his plate aside, stepped into the middle of the assembly and announced himself:

"General Guido Granelli, from Milano. Need anything more be said?"

As he stepped back to resume his repast, there was a brief round of hand-clapping led by Anton Ziegler. All eyes fixed with respect and a degree of awe on the military figure so evidently conscious of his own importance. Following the introductions, they broke up again into smaller groups, Anton Ziegler button-holing the security expert and Pignatelli engaging the lady professor. Guido Granelli held himself a little aloof, while the count uncorked more wine and did the rounds, like a good host, refilling glasses.

When the hands of the wall-clock eventually moved towards ten fifteen, Count Flavio again broke up lively conversations that assured him that the group was melding well, to announce:

"Ladies and gentlemen, our arrangement with the hotel requires us to vacate the Functions Room in fifteen minutes. We shall reconvene tomorrow at this very spot immediately after lunch, to allow you time in the morning to explore this beautiful city. Meanwhile, I bid you all a good night's rest."

"*Buona notte*," they all chimed in chorus, already beginning to disperse to their private rooms; except for Count Flavio, who drew Anton Ziegler confidentially to one side.

"Excellent wine," Ziegler remarked, obsequiously. "From your own estates, I gather?"

"Comparable with the best Soaves, in our humble opinion," the other replied, with mock modesty. "Now that I've met you, Herr Ziegler, there is a little matter I wish to raise with you ahead of tomorrow's conference."

"Regarding funding?" the Swiss enquired, attentively.

Count Flavio nodded.

"I have collected a fair sum of money from various sources in Italy," he explained.

"Legitimate sources?" Ziegler asked, with heavy irony.

The count returned a rather enigmatic smile.

"Many activities of rather questionable provenance take place these days," he said, "in Italy as in other countries."

"Such as?"

"Clandestine excavation from archaeological sites," the count went on, "is one of our particular problems. Valuable figurines, vases and amphorae from the Greek and Etruscan periods go missing regularly, to be smuggled out of the country. They often end up in American museums, few questions asked. Why, only last month a Greek psykter from the sixth century BC was stolen from a traveling exhibition in Calabria. Luckily it was recovered, crated with a small Phoenician sculpture, in the port of Genoa."

The Swiss's features registered puzzlement.

"A psykter is an ancient wine cooler," the count explained. "Don't you think the ancients liked their wine chilled on warm Mediterranean days?"

"Excuse my ignorance," the other said, fully appreciating Greek ingenuity. "Rare books is more my line of country. But tell me, your funds surely did not originate from such illegal activities?"

"I accepted donations to our cause from a variety of sources," Flavio replied, sotto voce. "And as far as I am concerned, they were just that—donations. Some of it was undoubtedly legitimate, from agricultural interests similar to my own, weary of EU intervention and meddling. As for the rest, I cared not to enquire too closely into sources. It would have been a pointless exercise, in any case."

"It's a pity," Ziegler said, "that we have to rely on devious methods to raise money for our cause. On the other hand, given the absolute secrecy required to achieve our objective, we can hardly ask the public for contributions, can we?"

The elderly aristocrat smiled his enigmatic smile.

"I see that you and I are of one mind," he observed. "In this matter, the end will have to justify the means."

"Precisely," agreed the Swiss. "And you now wish to transfer this sum to my safe-keeping?"

"I have a close family friend in Zurich," the count explained. "On your doorstep, as it happens; which is just as well. Actually, she is the daughter of a childhood friend now living in America. She is holding the funds for me in the account of the school where she is employed as registrar and burser. She's a reliable girl, name of Jill Crabtree."

"It was wise to ship the funds out of Italy," Ziegler said, "to stave off enquiries."

"The Carabinieri are keen as mustard these days, as regards any form of money laundering. I could not be one hundred per cent certain that they would not eventually trace some questionable monies to me, if I held them in an Italian bank account."

"So I can expect Fraulein Crabtree to contact me?" the Swiss enquired.

"I'll get her to give you a call, soon as I get back to the Villa Serena."

"At Buchhandlung Anton Ziegler, on the Niederdorf," the other explained. "I'll give you my phone number after tomorrow's session. Sleep well, my dear Count."

"*Gleichfalls*," the other replied, in his best German. "I wish you the same."

chapter 10

SATURDAY MORNING DAWNED fine and clear, promising a beautiful June day. After breakfast, George Mason left his hotel, crossed the bridge by the Water Church and strolled down the opposite bank of the Limmat to the Hauptbahnhof. The station was as busy as ever, travelers arriving from and departing to all corners of Europe at this height of the tourist season. On arrival, he approached the bookstall and bought a copy of the London *Times*, to catch up on news from England and the county cricket scores, noting with satisfaction that Yorkshire had a first innings lead over neighboring Lancashire in the Roses match, so-named for continuing on the sports field the rivalry between the White Rose and the Red that had embroiled his medieval countrymen in a series of civil wars extending over a hundred years. That the Lancastrians had eventually prevailed had always been a rather sore point with the detective, a proud Yorkshireman; hence it invariably pleased him when his home side defeated them on the field. He turned next to the Business Section, to check the performance of the few stocks he and Adele held in joint names.

Rolf Kubler was expecting him by pre-arranged appointment when he entered the nearby Polizei Dienst around eleven o'clock, having lingered for a short while over coffee at the station buffet. The lieutenant, engaged in clearing his desk ahead of the weekend break, rose to greet him.

"*Guten Tag, Herr Inspektor,*" he said expansively, offering him a chair.

"A fine morning it is, too," George Mason responded. "Thinking of taking a cruise down the lake after lunch, perhaps as far as Rapperswil."

"And I aim to do a spot of trout fishing on a tributary of the Sihl," Kubler said, evidently relishing the prospect. "Meanwhile, there's something you might like to mull over while enjoying the lake air."

"Developments?" the detective asked, sitting bolt upright.

"Regarding your choir friend, Mr Max Fifield."

"The special audit at Manfred Bott AG has already been completed?"

"I received their report late yesterday afternoon. Max Fifield's field trips do, in fact, tally with the approximate dates of the missing books."

"You don't say so!" Mason exclaimed.

"He was definitely in Konstanz around the time Ackerman's *The History of Westminster Abbey* disappeared."

He paused for a moment to gauge the effect of his words on his visitor, noting the gleam of triumph in his eye.

"And he was also, according to Manfred Bott's sales records, visiting Luino around the time Palladio's *Architettura* went missing; as well as being in Winterthur when the Mozart piano score was purloined."

"We already know," the detective said, "that he called at Schaffhausen Polytechnic recently. It's beginning to appear that we can build some sort of case at last. Harrington will be over the moon."

The Swiss lieutenant was more circumspect.

"What we have, my dear Inspector Mason, is certainly very curious and interesting. But it is, in fact, nothing more than a coincidence of dates. Or rather, a coincidence of approximate dates, since nobody can be sure of the exact day the items went missing."

"You mean there was a time-lag between their disappearance and the discovery of the thefts by college authorities?"

"Precisely," returned Kubler.

George Mason pondered the situation, as his opposite number added his signature to some items of police correspondence, to get outstanding business cleared by noon, so that he could concentrate on fly-fishing.

"What it amounts to," Mason eventually said, "is circumstantial evidence. We need something more concrete, to pin Fifield down. I personally am now convinced beyond a reasonable doubt that he is involved in all this."

"That might be more easily said than done," the Swiss cautioned. "According to Kaporal Goetz, the student Erik Muntener is sticking to his story that he intended to dispose of the article on the Internet. His case comes before the court in mid-July."

"So what do you suggest?" Mason asked, hoping that the lieutenant, from his store of police experience, would have some useful ideas.

Rolf Kubler sat back in his swivel-chair, folded his arms across his chest and gave a knowing smile.

"It would be advantageous," he said, "if at this stage we could catch him, if not exactly red-handed, then the next best thing."

"And how do you propose to do that?" a skeptical Mason asked.

"We could do a thorough search of his apartment," Kubler replied. "Alfons Goetz can lead a small, highly-trained team in there, vet the premises and leave absolutely no trace of their visit. If we find even one of the missing items, we've hit the jackpot."

George Mason rose from his seat and crossed to the window, which overlooked the railway yards, his eye caught momentarily by a long, dark-blue sleeper train pulling into the Hauptbahnhof. Turning back to Kubler, he said:

"I can suggest the perfect occasion for it," he announced.

"Indeed?" the other said, crossing the room to join him by the window. He too liked to watch trains.

"On Wednesday evenings, he invariably attends choir practice at St Wilfrid's. Starts promptly at 7 p.m."

"The sooner the better," Kubler said. "We'll make it this coming Wednesday. I'll alert Kaporal Goetz first thing Monday morning to get his team in place. By the way, that's the night train from Prague just pulling in."

"The one with the wagons-lit?" Mason asked, recognizing in the lieutenant a fellow railway buff.

Kubler nodded. "Now, if you'll excuse me, Inspector Mason," he said, "I have just a few small matters to clear up before I can start my weekend. I'll contact you directly anything turns up."

❦

The weather in Ticino was not so fine as farther north, beyond the alps. A low-pressure system was moving in across the Dolomites, bringing steady rain. The members of the inner circle of Amadeo were glad to take an early lunch in the dining-room of Hotel Papavero, anxious to get down to the day's business. By 1.30 pm, they were already seated round an oval mahogany table in the Functions Room, where they were served black coffee and grappa, before the waiting staff withdrew and the doors were sealed by Giulietta Ferrara. Count Flavio de Montesedina distributed the photocopies Marco Villanuova had prepared for him in the college music department and opened the proceedings.

"I propose a toast," he announced, "to our model and inspiration, Amadeo d'Alassio."

The small assembly rose to their feet, raised their tots of grappa and proclaimed in loud voices:

"Amadeo d'Alassio!"

Still standing, they replaced their empty glasses on the table, took up their music sheets and sang in unison, if not quite in tune, an opera aria made famous by the celebrated tenor Luciano Pavarotti, Verdi's *Nessun Dorma*. Seemingly well-pleased with their efforts, they repeated the performance, exchanged smiles of satisfaction and gave each other polite handclaps.

"That should set the tone for the meeting quite nicely," the gratified aristocrat said, as they resumed their seats. "First item on the agenda is Herr Ziegler's report on finance."

The Swiss antiquarian cleared his throat and said:

"For those of you who are not familiar with the need to raise a considerable amount of money, an operational fund as it were, let me explain. General Granelli informed *Il Direttore* at the outset of this enterprise that he could not count on the support of key junior officers without offering them substantial bribes."

A murmur of indignation, rather than surprise, rippled through the group.

"Fund-raising activities have been entrusted to just two members of the inner circle, myself and Count Flavio, and have been on-going for a period of several months. I can report that we shall have, by the end of June, sufficient monies to cover all foreseeable expenses. A buyer from the United States, from Philadelphia in fact, will then be meeting with Herr Ziegler regarding the purchase of rare books to the value of, approximately, 200,000 euros. Count Flavio's efforts among sympathizers in northern Italy have raised nearly half as much again."

This announcement was greeted with murmurs of approval and a rapping of hands on the bare mahogany.

"Let me add," Ziegler went on, "that my own efforts have been very ably supported by a member of the Britannia Party of Great Britain, whose general aims are consistent with our own. We owe him a great debt of gratitude."

"Who is this individual?" Alessandro Pignatelli wanted to know.

"For the present," the Swiss answered, in conclusion, "that individual must remain anonymous."

Count Flavio thanked him warmly and turned to the person on his immediate left.

"General?"

The military man took a deep breath and braced his shoulders.

"Now for the nitty-gritty," he said. "On the morning of July 10th, my brigade will surround the Parliament building. A platoon led by myself shall enter the chamber, arrest the prime minister and declare the Socialist government void. The prime minister and his entire cabinet shall then be placed under arrest. As a temporary measure, we hope."

"What about the media?" Ilona Rosso enquired.

"I've already thought of that," the general said. "Additional small units of alpinisti will occupy the main television stations and instruct newscasters to announce that a coup d'etat has taken place and that a new government headed by General Guido Granelli has been formed, with immediate effect. Everything should go like clockwork. We don't want any slip-ups, as in the abortive coup against the Spanish government in 1981 or the attempted strike against French premier, Pierre Mendes-France, back in 1955."

"Can you count absolutely on the loyalty of your junior officers and the rank-and-file?" Pignatelli enquired, with concern.

"Absolutely," Guido replied. "Their loyalty is to me personally."

"But your brigade is based near Milan, isn't it?" the count remarked. "Isn't that a far cry from the main centers of power?"

The general smiled his rather condescending smile.

"By routine rotation of troops," he said, airily, "the 5th Light Infantry are due to move into the Rome command region at the end of this month. We shall then have sole responsibility for the security of the city of Rome and its environs."

"So you will be the only military personnel within a hundred miles of the capital?" the count said, with satisfaction.

"Precisely."

"Professore Rosso?" prompted Count Flavio, turning next to the person on his right.

"The first act of the new government," Ilona Rosso said, "will be to name a new cabinet and replace the chief officers of state, in the civil service and the judiciary, with our own nominees. Our next priority will be to start negotiations leading to withdrawal from the Maastricht Treaty. Italy shall once again become a fully autonomous state, responsible for its own affairs without being dictated to by an outsize bureaucracy in Brussels. We owe it to the memory of Giuseppe Garibaldi, Amadeo d'Alassio and the countless others who fought for the unification of our historic country several generations ago."

"Hear, hear!" chimed the group, in unison, while rapping the table loudly with the palms of their hands.

"July 10th, as it happens," Flavio said, "is also the anniversary of the birth of Amadeo d'Alassio."

"By design or by coincidence?" asked Pignatelli.

"By design," the general said, emphatically. "It also happens to be the last-but-one date on which the parliament meets before the long summer recess. The delegates will be contemplating vacations in the mountains or by the sea. They will be taken completely off-guard."

The conference continued through most of the afternoon, to rehearse thoroughly the roles of each of the key participants, to iron out numerous minor details and to confirm the date of their final meeting at Turin. At 4 p.m, Count Flavio brought proceedings to a close with the announcement of a formal dinner to be held that evening at the Ristorante Rimini just outside town, on the Bellinzona road. It was an establishment that specialized in the cuisine and vintages of the Abruzzi region and had been recommended as a fitting venue to celebrate anticipated success by no less a person than *Il Direttore* who, unfortunately, was unable to attend.

On the Sunday evening, around the same time that Count Flavio arrived back at his villa in Stresa, Jill Crabtree heard the doorbell chime at her small apartment in central Zurich. She was just adding the final touches to table settings for four, having invited her close friends in St Wilfrid's choir to dinner, following a long-standing custom that they each occasionally invite the others home, as a change from dining out in restaurants. Setting a vase of carnations in the center as a final touch, she smoothed her dress and went to answer the summons. A smiling Margaret Fern and Hugh Selby entered, the former presenting her with a bottle of Burgundy, the latter with chocolate truffles.

"Max will be along shortly," Hugh assured her, accepting the offer of a seat on the compact divan, which doubled as a bed. "He has to prepare some materials for his field trip tomorrow."

Margaret Fern remained standing, hovering near the small kitchen in case she could be of assistance.

"Oh, do sit down Meg," Jill said. "I'll just pop the meat back in the fridge. Nothing will spoil even if Max is, as usual, running late."

"What's on the menu?" Hugh enquired, eyeing the tastefully arranged dining-table with approval and interest.

"Fondue bourguignonne," the hostess replied, evidently very pleased with her latest culinary venture, culled from a French cookery book her mother had recently sent her.

The two guests exchanged meaningful smiles; they were accustomed by now to the lead soprano coming up with the unexpected.

"Must have involved a deal of preparation," Margaret said, genuinely impressed and occupying the seat next to the young man.

"On the contrary," Jill replied, breezily. "It's you who'll be doing all the work, as you shall soon see. Now what will you both have to drink?"

"A dry Martini," Hugh said, at once.

"I'll have a gin-and-tonic," Margaret answered.

"Coming up," their hostess said, crossing to the small cocktail cabinet on the far wall, as her guests took in the details of the room.

"I see you've bought a new picture," Margaret said, indicating the Matisse still-life behind the dining-table.

"It's only a print," Jill modestly explained. "But I think it goes very nicely in the dining area."

"Very appropriate," Hugh said. "It fits in well with your other paintings, the Cezanne and the Klimt."

"And it complements your color scheme," Margaret said.

Jill poured herself a Campari and occupied an armchair facing her guests. The hands of the ebony wall-clock had moved on to 7.20.

"Max is already twenty minutes late," she remarked. "He might at least have rung."

"Perhaps we should start without him," Margaret suggested.

Jill tended to agree.

"Tell you what," she said, "I'll start putting things out, while you two finish your drinks. It will take a little time and he'll probably show up by then. He enjoys a good meal."

That said, she repaired to the kitchen and soon reappeared with a table burner, over which she placed a small copper vat of olive oil. She lit the burner and adjusted the flame to a low setting, returned to the kitchen and brought out a tray holding several round porcelain dishes much like soup bowls, containing vegetables, pickles and savories. These she placed in a circular arrangement around the burner. Last of all, she emerged with a large plate of raw beef, cut into cubes. The whole process took less than fifteen minutes.

"Dinner is served," she announced, with a gleam of triumph in her eye.

As her bemused guests downed their drinks and approached the novel spread, the doorbell rang again.. The hostess sprang to open it, ushering a very apologetic Max

Fifield into the company. He warmly greeted the others, as they all sat at table.

"And what do we have here?" he asked skeptically, as Jill uncorked the wine Margaret Fern had brought and half filled the glasses.

"Fondue bourguignonne," Jill replied. "It's a recipe my mother sent me."

"What do we do exactly?" Hugh enquired, rather tentatively.

"It's quite straightforward," their hostess replied, testing the temperature of the oil with the tip of her finger. "Serve yourselves liberally from the side dishes, skewer cubes of beef with your fork and lower them into the cooking oil until done as you prefer—rare, medium-rare or well-done. Enjoy!"

Much intrigued, the trio of guests did as instructed and were soon settled into a most enjoyable meal, at which each was his own chef.

"Where's George?" Hugh Selby eventually asked.

Jill and Max exchanged glances, the latter's face darkening somewhat at the mention of the Yorkshireman's name.

"I was a bit undecided about whether to include him," Jill said, frankly. "And in the end I decided not to, mainly because he's only here short-term."

"Quite right," Max Fifield said, approvingly. "It's not as if he's really one of us."

"More wine?" the hostess asked, to fill an awkward pause.

"The Nuits St Georges goes admirably with the beef fondue," Hugh said, enthusiastically. "A good choice, Meg. I for one would like a refill."

134

At that, all four glasses nudged forward, calling for the opening of a second red of lesser vintage, a Beaujolais Villages.

"We did already invite him to the Wienerwald," Margaret said, bathing in Hugh Selby's compliment.

"I'm not sure that I care for him all that much," Max announced abruptly, while skewering a fresh cube of beef and cooking it to medium-rare.

"I disagree," asserted Margaret. "I like his rather dry sense of humor."

"Don't you mean sarcasm?" Max countered.

Ignoring that quip, the young woman went on to explain how interested George Mason seemed in her charity work, particularly in the plight of young women caught up in the sex trade and in the hostel they were building for their safety at Debrecen.

"He's a decent enough old stick," Hugh put in. "I don't dislike him, but he's not really our age-group, is he?"

They continued their meal in silence for a while. The heap of raw beef cubes steadily diminished, as did the pickled walnuts, olives, salad items and wild rice. The hostess inwardly complimented herself on a notable culinary success as she skipped briefly to the kitchen to extract the dessert, a home-made blueberry cheesecake, from the fridge.

Pushing his dinner plate aside, with a sigh of satisfaction, Max suddenly asked:

"Do you think George Mason is all he claims to be?"

"What on earth do you mean?" Margaret Fern challenged, at once.

"All this business about scouting for a tour company, for one thing," the other retorted. "Doesn't ever say very much about his findings, does he?"

"I know for a fact that he's very keen to attend the Pergolesi Festival," his defender said. "I've mentioned it to him a couple of times and he's really interested."

"Are you saying he's not what he appears to be, Max?" an astonished Hugh Selby asked.

"He just doesn't fit the image of the tour industry," Max declared, emphatically.

"I tend to agree with you," Jill said. "To me, he seems more like an official of some kind. An Inland Revenue inspector maybe. Something like that."

"You mean he's here to check up on us, in case we're evading income tax?" the young tenor quipped.

"Do be serious, Hugh," Margaret objected. Turning to Max Fifield she said, rather sarcastically, "Aren't you letting your imagination run away with you?"

The book salesman raised his hands in a mock-defensive gesture and left it at that. Time would tell, he thought to himself, nervously toying with his wineglass.

The hostess, to create a diversion now that their plates were empty, interjected:

"I think it's time we had some dessert."

The proposal was met with a murmur of approval as she extinguished the burner and commenced clearing the table, firmly refusing offers of help from Margaret Fern. In no time at all, blueberry cheesecake and fresh coffee made their appearance.

"Why don't you put on that CD you brought with you, Hugh?" she asked, indicating the Sony equipment on the bookcase.

"Which one is that?" Max enquired.

"Vaughan Williams's song-cycle *On Wenlock Edge*," the tenor replied, "sung by Simon Keenlyside."

"That's a capital idea," Margaret said. "We can listen to it while finishing dinner."

"When you've had your desssert, why don't you all transfer to the easy chairs with your coffee. I have some champagne cognac to go with it."

They soon complied, filling out a pleasant evening without further altercation or disagreement on the subject of a portly, middle-aged gentleman from the north of England, alternating between conversation about parish and choral matters and listening to CDs, including one or two from Jill's varied collection, her own favorite being the jazz saxophone of John Coltrane. Rising to leave at ten-thirty ahead of an early start the next day, Max asked to borrow Hugh's recording. The other two followed soon afterwards, leaving their hostess with a minimal amount of clearing up to do and a sink full of dishes to wash.

She was part-way through this task, humming to herself one of the tunes from a CD, when the telephone rang. Thinking it was one of her guests who had perhaps left something behind, she was quite surprised on lifting the receiver to hear the rather gravely voice of her mother's old friend, Count Flavio de Montesedina.

"Good evening, Jill," he began. "I hope it's not too late to call. Just got back from an important meeting at Lugano."

"Why, hello!" Jill responded. "This is a surprise. I was just tidying up after a small dinner party, before going to bed."

"Sounds like an enjoyable evening."

"It went very well," she replied. " I served my first-ever fondue bourguignonne."

"Congratulations, Jill. Now listen carefully," he said, his tone hardening. "The funds you have been holding for me in your school account must now be handed over without delay to a Herr Anton Ziegler."

"Anton Ziegler," Jill repeated, to make sure she had got the name right.

"He runs a bookshop at the lake end of the Niederdorf. You can't miss it. Has his name over the window. He's
expecting you any day now."

"Will do," she promised.

"Good night, Jill, and take care."

Replacing the receiver, she jotted the name down on a
notepad in order not to forget it and returned to the kitchen
to dry dishes, feeling a keen sense of relief that this matter,
which had caused her some anxiety over the past few weeks,
would soon be over. She would withdraw the money from
the bursar's account, she decided, the very next day, confident that in the short time it had resided there no one had
noticed the temporary boost to school funds. She nearly
had kittens the day staff from the Kantonal Taxburo turned
up to conduct a special audit, but since no issues had been
raised as a result, she put it down to one of those routine
spot inspections they were accustomed to doing any time it
pleased them, at any business premises. The International
School, being privately funded, was a business like any other. Completing her chores, she poured herself a nightcap
from her flask of Remy Martin, sat back on the divan and
mused over the evening's events. Of particular interest to
her was Max's attitude towards George Mason. She had noticed the way his face had darkened at the mention of the
Yorkshireman's name. Max Fifield and Count Flavio were
evidently into something. Whether it was legitimiate or il-
legitimate, she chose not to consider. Yet the notion nagged
at her, as she undressed and converted the divan into a low
bed, that it might just possibly have something to do with
George Mason. If she was perfectly honest with herself, she
did not really think Mason was involved in the tour business
either; yet what a find he had been for St Wilfrid's choir.
Even Max acknowledged that he was a first-class bass.

chapter 11

FIRST THING MONDAY morning, Signore Pollini left his office at Succor in the Oerlikon district of Zurich and caught the tram as far as the Hauptbahnhof. On alighting, he crossed a lawned area behind the station, thinly screened by a stand of sycamores from the railway yards, in good time for his appointment with Leutnant Rolf Kubler. The latter was speaking on the telephone as the charity director was shown into his private office. The Swiss, motioning vigorously with his free arm for his visitor to take a seat, continued his conversation for a few moments before firmly replacing the receiver and rising to greet his visitor.

"*Guten Tag*, Herr Pollini," he said, stretching out his palm across the cluttered desk.

The visitor rose and firmly shook his hand.

"Now regarding your friend, Laszlo Polke," Kubler began.

The director was all attention, clasping his hands at the knee rather tensely.

"You suspect him of misdirecting funds destined for the construction of a hostel for young women in Hungary? A case of embezzlement, to put it bluntly."

"And you have made some enquiries?" Pollini asked, expectantly.

"Nothing too promising for the moment," the Swiss replied. "Except that Kaporal Goetz has discovered he had strong right-wing affiliations during his time at university."

The charity director returned a puzzled look.

"What can that possibly have to do with anything?" he asked, petulantly.

The lieutenant sat back in his chair and tapped his fingers on the desk, weighing his words carefully. Eventually he explained, without mentioning Mason by name:

"A certain colleague of mine, who is working on a different case, has done some research on nationalist organizations in former Warsaw Pact countries. This, as part of a wider enquiry he has been engaged in for some time."

"Tell me more," said the other, much intrigued.

"My colleague seems to think that there is some sort of right-wing movement afoot involving certain individuals in this city and perhaps beyond. This highly-experienced agent would not go so far as to call it a conspiracy, at least not yet. But what we do know is that quite substantial sums of money are being bandied about. To what end, we just don't know."

Signore Pollini's brow puckered, as he thought he saw what the police lieutenant was driving at.

"You are implying," he said, "that my young employee, Laszlo Polke, may be diverting funds from our charity to some kind of political agenda?"

"There is a very active one in Hungary, his country of origin," Kubler explained. "Goes by the name of Zeged. Its main platform is to oppose pro-western groups who favor applying for membership of the European Union. Quite a small organization, apparently. Probably in need of financial support."

"I was aware that Laszlo's father moved to Switzerland from Hungary during the Uprising, and that he had been a noted freedom fighter there."

"That is something I was not aware of," Kubler said. "It seems clear, however, from what you say, that there is a tradition of strong nationalist sentiment in the Polke family."

"And you think Laszlo could have inherited this?"

"It's all pure specualtion at the moment," the other said. "What we really need is firm evidence."

"And how do you propose to come by that?" asked the skeptical director.

The Swiss rose from his desk, crossed to his filing cabinet and drew out a folder. Opening it, he said:

"The main agency for transfers of money from Switzerland to East European countries is Balaton Bank, in Lausanne."

"Can you check if Laszlo has made deposits there in recent weeks?"

Leutnant Kubler shook his head.

"Not with the information we have to go off so far," he said. "There is just not enough indication of criminal intent to penetrate our banking secrecy laws."

"Then we are stumped, I'm afraid," Pollini said, disappointedly.

"Not necessarily," the other replied. "We can ask Interpol to look into things at the receiving end. The head office of Balaton Bank is in Budapest. They can very likely obtain information on recent bank transfers from Lausanne."

Signore Pollini was visibly relieved.

"Let me know at once," he requested, rising to take his leave, "the moment anything of that nature comes to light."

"I'll gladly do that, Herr Pollini," Kubler promised.

Laszlo Polke had decided to take one of his vacation days. Rising a bit later than usual, he greeted Frau Genucchi on his way out, strode quickly down into the street from his second-floor apartment at Heldenstrasse 2 and made, as was his custom, for the Culman restaurant for a light breakfast. Digesting the main news items in *Tages Anzeiger* along with his coffee and rolls, he was more preoccupied with an e-mail message he had received two days ago from Tomas Vasaryk, his contact in Budapest. His Hungarian mentor had instructed him to make contact with a certain Anton Ziegler, whom he had described as a prominent member of a right-wing organization whose aims closely mirrored those of Zeged. Nationalist groups were, in Tomas's view, becoming increasingly marginalized at this time of growing European integration and there was a lot to be gained from closer cooperation and mutual support, where practicable. Laszlo himself was skeptical. To his mind, the general political atmosphere and operating conditions in one country were markedly different from those in another, particularly when comparing nations in Western Europe with members of the former Warsaw Pact. Switzerland, keen on retaining full autonomy, had chosen to remain aloof from the European Union altogether, while enjoying certain trading benefits. Of what possible use could an antiquarian book dealer on the Niederdorf be to an organization like Zeged? It was mainly to humor Tomas and his cronies, particularly the academic element among them who spent their lives inside ivory towers, that he had decided to pay Herr Ziegler a visit.

Lingering for a while over a refill of coffee to watch part of a television recording of an international soccer match, it was already mid-morning by the time he left the Culman. He commenced walking down Ramistrasse towards Belle Vue, from where it was just a short stroll to the

Niederdorf. Being one of Zurich's main arteries, the traffic even at this slack hour was quite heavy, with trams accelerating down the long, straight incline towards the lake. Laszlo liked to watch the trams. All cities, to his mind, should have a tramway system, and it had pleased him to read in the newspapers how some places in England, such as Manchester and Sheffield, were reintroducing them after a long absence. They helped cut down on motor vehicles and urban pollution. In his private utopia, cars and trucks would be banned altogether from city centers, to be replaced by mass-transit systems.

It concerned him a little as he walked that Tomas made no reference to the transfer he had recently made through Balaton Bank in Lausanne. Perhaps that was merely down to caution on his mentor's part, but he still thought that some form of cryptic acknowledgement might have been made, just to let him know that the funds had arrived safely. He was taking a considerable risk and, to avoid arousing suspicion among his colleagues at Succor, it would be some months before he could make a second transfer, ahead of the referendum on joining the European Union scheduled for later that year. Zeged would do its utmost to stall, and if possible to prevent, any application for membership. Hungary could then remain like Switzerland and Norway, enjoying trade benefits while retaining full independence.

His thoughts turned to Meg Fern, as she was known at the office. She was, he estimated, a few years his senior and, as far as he was aware, unattached. He had always enjoyed a good working relationship with her and appreciated her dedication to the work in hand. What was merely a bread-and-butter job to him was to Meg akin to a vocation, perhaps from her sharing the same sex as the individuals they were aiming to help. Working closely with someone like that gave good insights into a person's character and interests.

He had begun to feel in recent months that he would like to get to know her better, outside the office environment. He thought of asking her out to dinner, but was afraid she might not accept, considering him perhaps too young, or too gauche. More worrying was that of late she had grown, if anything, more distant towards him, and he had been hard put to come up with a reason. The best explanation at the moment seemed to be that, with feminine intuition, she had divined the drift of his feelings towards her and was trying in a tactful way to discourage him. He was aware that she had many social contacts in Zurich, especially at St Wilfrid's church; it was quite possible that there was some-one in the background whom, for reasons best known to herself, she had kept quiet about at work.

It was close to midday by the time he reached the book-shop fronting the little square just behind the Niederdorf, which at that hour was full of tourists visiting the quaint boutiques and gourmet restaurants. Opening the door, he stepped cautiously inside, not quite knowing what sort of reception to expect. A tall, balding gentleman, seeing the young man as a potential buyer, emerged from behind the counter to greet him.

"Oleg Leverkov, at your service," he announced, brisk-ly.

"I wish to speak with the proprietor," Laszlo said, rath-er formally.

"Herr Anton Ziegler? Be kind to wait one moment."

He disappeared momentarily through the warren of small, interconnecting rooms lined floor to ceiling with musty bookshelves. He soon reappeared, closely followed by a shorter, elderly man with a wispy goatee, and resumed his position at the counter. The proprietor, accustomed to dealing with wealthy collectors, eyed the younger man with skepticism.

"What can I do for you, Herr…?" he asked.

"Polke," the other explained. "Laszlo Polke. I believe we have some special interests in common. Is there somewhere we can talk more privately?" He glanced pointedly at Leverkov, who was engrossed in a catalog, seemingly unaware of the visitor.

"I take it you are not here on book business," Ziegler said, testily. Yet something about the young man's demeanor prompted him to add: "I was just about to take a spot of lunch at the café across the square. If you would care to join me?"

"Gladly," Laszlo replied, at once. "But coffee will do fine. Had a late breakfast barely two hours ago."

"What did you say your name was, again?" Ziegler asked, on their way out.

"Laszlo Polke. My mentor at Zeged suggested that I contact you, and since this is one of my days off…"

"Isn't that some sort of nationalist organization?" the Swiss interrupted, his interest quickening. "By all means tell me more about it."

⋈

Jill Crabtree had decided on an early lunch-hour. She called first at the branch the Commerce Bank nearest the school, then caught a tram to Belle Vue. She did not pay much attention to two gentlemen in close conversation heading towards the café at the far side of the square, as she rounded the corner from the Niederdorf and walked tentatively up to the entrance of the antiquarian bookshop. Soon satisfied that these were the very premises Count Flavio had in mind for delivery of the funds he had entrusted to her keeping, she strode purposefully inside. Greeted at once by Oleg Leverkov, she took a step back, expecting an older man. The assistant seemed to sense her quandary.

"If it's Herr Ziegler you're after," he informed her, "he's just now gone off to lunch. Call back in an hour's time and you'll be sure to catch him."

"*Danke*," the young bursar said, with a tinge of disappointment. It meant that she would be late back in the afternoon and would have to think up some suitable excuse. Her priority now, she considered with a quick glance at her shoulder-bag, was to dispose of this money once and for all and regain her peace of mind.

She left the shop and strolled back towards the Niederdorf, bought a ham roll and a small Perrier from a street vendor and sat down on the steps by the cathedral to enjoy her snack and watch the tourist boats plying up and down the Limmat, past the elegant waterfront buildings. The tourist season was reaching its peak and the Romanesque cathedral to her left was one of the main attractions, evidenced by the frequent exclamations of fellow-Americans seeing it for the first time close-up and the clicking of Japanese cameras. It occurred to her that she had never actually been inside the noble, twin-spired edifice. With forty more minutes to kill and feeling a need to escape the midday heat, she made for the side entrance and stepped in beneath the low lintel.

The coolness of the large interior greeted her like an evening breeze. Yet how plain and simple it was, with its polished oak pews and carved pulpit. What a contrast to the Jesuit church at Lucerne, certainly one of the most beautifully decorated buildings she had ever visited. Here, the beauty lay in simplicity and the complete absence of ornament, as if waiting to be filled by some other-worldly presence. Having completed a brief tour of the side aisles, she took a seat in a front pew and listened to the organist starting a rehearsal of what sounded to her like a Bach fugue, though it might just as easily have been by Buxtehude or Telemann, for all she knew. The swell of sound filled the building, soon quieting the chattering voices. Sunlight streamed through the incredibly beautiful modern stained-glass, the cathedral's sole concession to religious art. Below the east window there was no altar, just a plain table. That puzzled Jill for a while. Her mother Sophia had raised her initially in the Catholic faith, where an altar and tabernacle were the main focus of all churches. Here the communion table seemed almost an after-thought, until she reflected that the Swiss Reformation was the most radical of all. Preaching was the main emphasis, witnessed by the prominent pulpit.

Unclasping her shoulder-bag and glancing inside to check the contents yet again, she felt in these surroundings a little ashamed of her guilty secret, as if she were one of the money-changers in the temple. The organ music soothed her qualms, reminding her of services at St Wilfrid's and the recitals given from time to time by Dr Hurlimann. She would be sure to mention to the retired professor that she had been here, since he would almost certainly know the resident organist, who may even have been one of his pupils. A glance at her watch told her that it was time to leave, if she was to make it back to school without too much delay. Reluctantly, she tore herself away from the impromptu concert before the fugue was finished. Within ten minutes, she had introduced herself to an elderly Swiss sporting a wispy goatee beard.

"My dear Miss Crabtree," Anton Ziegler began genially, leading her at once to his private office at the rear of the labyrinthine premises, "I've been expecting you any day. No doubt, everything is in order?"

"I received a phone call from Count Flavio only yesterday evening," Jill replied. "I though it best to act without delay."

"You did right," the Swiss assured her. "Time is of the essence. Now tell me a little about youself. I understand that your relationship with the count goes back quite a long way."

"My mother and he were close childhood friends," Jill said, watching as he transferred the large-denomination bills to his safe with his customary sangfroid.

"You have performed a most valuable service to us," he assured her. "And for that, I am extremely grateful. If I can return the favor in any way, while you are living in Zurich, do not hesitate to ask. I have powerful friends here."

The thought crossed her mind that the antiquarian might in some way be able to help her obtain the type of property she was interested in, since properties in good residential areas were difficult to come by, without contacts. She filed the thought away in her mind, for future reference.

"I'll certainly do that," she said, taking her leave. "Must hurry now, or I'll be very late back at work."

"Then, not so much good bye," he remarked, genially, "as *Auf wiedersehen.*"

"*Auf wiedersehen*, Herr Ziegler," Jill replied, now feeling much more at ease about this whole enterprise, but extremely glad to have unloaded the money.

The Swiss followed her to the shop entrance and waved to her as she turned the corner into the Niederdorf. A quick skip down the narrow alley leading past L'Escargot, a restaurant serving roasted snails, would bring her to the tram stop on the Limmatquai.

chapter 12

GEORGE MASON SPENT most of Monday morning in his hotel room, reviewing the few developments in the case and faxing an interim summary to Chief Inspector Harrington. In the absence of a great deal of hard facts to report, he embellished what little material he had gathered, to give his superior officer the impression that steady progress was being made. Harrington was a man who expected results from the investment of police time and resources, and the last thing Mason wanted at this juncture was a recall to London. If to his chief this was merely a question of stolen books, to George Mason the case was taking on much wider implications, if only he could put his finger more exactly on what those were. Extreme right-wing politics were at the forefront of his mind. The Britannia Party, through Max Fifield, were almost certainly involved. Then there was Laszlo Polke and the curious Zeged organization. Last but not least came Anton Ziegler, whose former pro-Nazi sympathies were well documented.

His paperwork completed, Mason went down to the hotel dining-room for a light lunch, before setting off on a walking tour of the old city that Zurchers called the Altstadt. This was the nucleus of the modern city, known to the Romans as Turicum. He discovered a warren of narrow alleys winding their way up to the tree-fringed Lindenhof, reached by flights of stone steps linking a series of cobbled squares where small fountains played. Occasionally, there was a young violinist hoping to eke out his student stipend with offerings from passing tourists. A brief glance at the open violin cases on the cobbles convinced him that such contributions were minimal. Feeling that the exercise might do him good, he climbed right to the top with the aid of the handrails and stood a little out of breath to enjoy the exhilarating views over the city's tiled rooftops to the lake beyond and its fringe of mountains to the south.

It was then that he noticed Leutnant Rolf Kubler sitting with his back towards him on a wooden bench on the far side of the Lindenhof. The detective reacted in some surprise, until he realized that the Polizei Dienst was barely ten minutes' walk away and that this was probably as likely a spot as any for a summer lunch-break. He approached unheeded from behind, soon observing that the Swiss lieutenant was indeed tackling a large salami roll, while reading a copy of *Tages Anzeiger*. A half-smoked cigar lay on the bench beside him, next to a bottle of Vichy water.

"So this is where you spend valuable police time, is it?" Mason quipped, confronting him.

Kubler sat bolt upright, in his surprise nearly dropping his sandwich. Almost immediately, a wry smile spread across his intelligent features.

"Why, if it isn't Inspector Mason," he exclaimed, starting to get awkwardly to his feet.

"Don't bother to get up," the other said. "And don't mind me at all. Enjoy your snack. I was just taking in some of the sights."

"For Bowland Tours?" Kubler quipped humorously, refolding his newspaper.

"One might say that," Mason said, appreciating the irony.

"Have a seat, why don't you? Already eaten lunch?"

The detective nodded curtly and sat down beside him, glancing at the headlines in the paper as the Swiss finished eating.

"I was on the point of contacting you," Kubler said, eventually.

"So soon?"

"The report from the Carabinieri came through late yesterday. But there is nothing specific. Jill Crabtree's Italian friend could be one of any number of individuals involved in racketeering of one kind or another."

"Such as?" Mason asked.

"The usual things. Drug peddling is a major problem, as in many other countries. Forgeries and money laundering rank fairly high as well."

The detective's face clouded; he had been hoping for something more definite.

"Aren't there more localized scams?" he enquired. "You know what I mean, things more identifiable with Italy."

"Their main problem is the export of archaeological finds. But that's a very specialized market, including thefts from collections and clandestine digs at excavation sites, of which there several of note, especially in the south. The Italian police have a special task force designed to track them down. Hundreds of thousands of dollars are involved annually."

"Jill's friend must have been involved in something nefarious," Mason observed. "Otherwise, why would he shelter money in her school account?"

"The Italians are continuing their enquiries," Kubler assured him, "and will let us know if anything turns up. But, from my previous dealings with them, I wouldn't count on quick results."

"There was an item in the newspaper recently," Mason said, "about an interesting olive oil scam."

"I hadn't seen that," the other said.

"According to what I read, some growers have been importing inexpensive nut oils from the Near East, blending them with home-grown olive oil and promoting the result as virgin grade."

Rolf Kubler gave his characteristic wry smile.

"Can't say that surprises me in the least," he remarked. "They've had problems with adulterated wines too, in the past. I expect the authorities will soon crack down on it, to safeguard the export market."

"Our Italian friend could be a grower of some kind," Mason suggested. "Either of vines or olives, probably living in northern Italy, within reasonable reach of Bellinzona."

"Kaporal Goetz, who overheard part of the conversation at the station buffet, was fairly confident the gentleman in question spoke with a vaguely Milanese accent."

"Then you should ask the Carabinieri to focus on the area between, say, Milan and Locarno, at the head of Lake Maggiore, covering all major towns in between."

"I can certainly do that," the Swiss agreed, rising to his feet and shaking the crumbs off his lap. "Must get back to headquarters now. The Kommandant is conducting a briefing promptly at two o'clock, about counteracting hooliganism on the Swiss National Day."

"I take it your corporal is all set up for Wednesday evening?" Mason enquired, picturing in his mind what to him seemed an unlikely scenario, that of drunks rampaging through the refined purlieus of the old city.

"The evening of the choir rehearsal," Kubler confirmed. "Absolutely. He has already put a small team together. I'll ring you at your hotel first thing Thursday morning, to let you know the results."

"I'll look forward to it," the detective said. *"Auf wiedersehen."*

"Bis Donnerstag," the other replied, walking briskly away. "Until Thursday."

⌖

When Thursday came, George Mason rose early and was soon down in the dining-room enjoying a breakfast of scrambled eggs and grilled ham, having eaten enough muesli to last him a good while. As he ate, he leafed through the hotel copy of *Tages Anzeiger* to catch up on the main news items, agreeably surprising himself at his increasing grasp of the German language. Laying the newspaper aside in order to pour his coffee, he mused on the events of the previous evening. The rehearsal of the Vaughan William's anthem had gone fairly well and Dr Hurlimann seemed very upbeat. Max Fifield, on the other hand, seemed markedly cooler towards him than on previous occasions, which led the detective to wonder if, by some incredible stroke of mischance, he had penetrated his cover. Sitting over their communal night-cap at Der Waldman afterwards, until the cuckoo clock sounded the hour of ten, Max had also made pointed references to his tour-scouting activities. He had been able to counter inuendos by describing his visit to the Altstadt on Monday afternoon and the trip he had made on Tuesday to Einsiedeln, a popular tourist destination less than an hour by rail from the Hauptbahnhof. The monastery there was noted for the shrine of the Black Madonna, Margaret Fern had informed him, as if to encourage his researches, and was popular with pilgrims. Hugh Selby and Jill Crabtree also still seemed to accept him at face value, if increasingly as a temporary member of their circle, who would most likely in the near future be departing Zurich.

"Herr Mason," the breakfast waiter suddenly said. "*Telefon.*"

The detective eased himself from his chair and crossed to the hotel lobby, expecting a call from Leutnant Kubler, while thinking it was a little early for that. Instead, he was greeted by the stentorian voice of Chief Inspector Harrington, calling from Scotland Yard.

"Good morning, Inspector," he began. "How's the weather down there?"

"A bit overcast, at the moment," his subordinate replied. "Rain expected later."

"Much like London then," Harrington said, gruffly. "Now listen carefully. I received your faxed progress report and frankly I'm not impressed. Have you actually achieved anything in the weeks you've been there?"

"It's not a simple case," Mason replied, a bit taken aback even though he had anticipated some such reaction on his senior's part. "There are ramifications."

"The Superintendant thinks you've been away long enough, and I tend to agree with him. To hell with ramifications. All you have to do is help solve the theft of a few old books."

"More easily said than done, Chief," Mason countered. "I've put in a deal of patient investigative work. Hoping for positive results any day now."

Harrington grunted dismissively.

"What about that chap Fifield I researched for you?" he asked. "Isn't he involved?"

"Almost certainly. But I need more evidence."

"Listen again. There's an urgent case come up in Knightsbridge that's just your line of country. The Superintendant wants you on it as soon as possible, to spearhead the investigation. Currently, for want of manpower, it's under a rookie, Detective Constable Myers. You've got until mid-July to wind things up in Zurich. Then you're on the first plane back. And, by the way, call in at one of those specialist chocolate boutiques they have down there before you leave. My wife Cynthia loves Swiss dark chocolate."

George Mason smiled to himself as he replaced the receiver. Behind all Harrington's gruff exterior there was a human heart after all. So he now had a deadline, he mused, returning to his table to finish his coffee; and it was less than two weeks away! Hopefully, Kubler would have good news for him. He had barely sat down when the waiter approached him again.

"Herr Mason," he requested. "*Bitte, am Telefon.*"

This could only be the lieutenant, he thought, eagerly expecting positive developments as he eased his portly frame once more from his chair and strode purposefully towards the lobby.

"*Guten Tag,* Inspector," came the more genial voice of the Swiss. "*Haben Sie gut geschlaffen?*"

"I slept very well, thanks," the detective replied. "Must be all the fresh air and exercise, getting round your fascinating city."

"Kaporal Goetz's team went in yesterday evening, as planned."

"And...?" asked Mason, eagerly.

"They drew a blank, I'm afraid. Fifield's apartment is clean. Clean as a whistle."

Mason said nothing for a few moments, absorbing the implications of this unexpected setback and suppressing feelings of keen disappointment.

"You still there?" Kubler asked, anxiously.

"Just taking stock, Lieutenant," he replied. "Look, I'm fairly certain Max Fifield's up to his neck in all this. Get onto Erik Muntener and see if you can crack him. Offer him a plea bargain, if possible, in exchange for his testimony. Chief Inspector Harrington is breathing down my neck. I need results fast."

"We'll do what we can," the Swiss assured him, sympathetically. "I'll put Alfons Goetz onto it straight away."

George Mason walked thoughtfully back to the dining-room and regained his place, allowing himself to be distracted by the table chatter of a group of Scottish tourists who had checked into the hotel the previous day. The musical sound of their broad Scottish brogue lifted his spirits, as he poured fresh coffee and took up his newspaper, determined not to let two negative phone calls interfere with his morning routine, in which the *Tages Anzeiger* had an essential place.

⌐≈⌐

Max Fifield, with some vacation time due to him, decided to take the day off work. After a hurried breakfast, he telephoned Anton Ziegler to arrange a meeting at ten o'clock at the Gruene Heinrich restaurant by Belle Vue, just a short walk from the antiquarian bookshop. The clouds had thickened by the time he boarded his tram and a light rain had begun to fall. No matter, he thought; they could just as well take their coffee inside the establishment as outdoors at the sidewalk tables. What a cool customer George Mason was, he reflected, as the tram headed smoothly towards Belle Vue. All that talk yesterday evening with Meg Fern about the Black Madonna at Einsiedeln, as if he really were a scout for a travel company in Clitheroe! He felt a grudging admiration for him, even if he had never really liked him personally. More to the point, how advanced was the Scotland Yard man's investigation into the books he had arranged to be taken from various university libraries over the past few months? And how advanced were Ziegler's plans to ship them overseas?

A traffic jam on Seefeldstrasse delayed him by fifteen minutes. Anton Ziegler was already seated at a quiet corner table skimming through a copy of *Zuri-Leu,* a popular tabloid, by the time Max entered the Heinrich.

"Haven't ordered yet," the Swiss explained. "What will you have, the Costa Rican or the Java? Both are very good."

"The Java, I think," Max said, taking his seat.

"Two Javas," Ziegler instructed the waitress, "with cream, but no sugar."

"Sorry I'm a bit late," Max apologized. "There was a minor collision involving two cars, just down the road from here. The police stopped all traffic."

Anton Ziegler folded his newspaper and laid it on the table beside him.

"Now tell me what's on your mind," he said, "that couldn't have waited until this evening?"

"You're not going to like this, Anton," the salesman began, clearing his throat. "My apartment was entered last evening, while I was out at choir practice."

"You mean it was burgled?" asked the elder man, sitting up in concern.

"I very much doubt it," the other replied, "since nothing was taken and the place was left as I always keep it, neat as a new pin."

"Then how do you know you had visitors?"

"Because of one small detail. Last Sunday evening, a fellow choir member lent me a CD of an English song-cycle. Before leaving for St Wilfrid's, I placed it on top of my CD player, expressly to remind me to listen to it before going to bed."

"And?"

"It was in a different position when I returned."

"Where was it then, in fact?" a rather perturbed Anton Ziegler asked.

"On the occasional table. Someone, perhaps curious about the title, must have picked it up to examine it and replaced it elsewhere, just a few feet away."

"And who do you suppose this someone might be?"

"I'll give you only one guess," Max said.

"George Mason?"

The salesman shook his head.

"He was at choir practice with me," he said. "But as I lay awake thinking about it last night, it occurred to me that Mason would certainly have known I'd be at the choir. Wednesday evening's a regular fixture."

Anton Ziegler sipped his coffee thoughtfully.

"My guess in that case would be the local police. If Mason is in cahoots with them, which is more than likely, it means that he knows about Muntener's arrest."

"Then he must also suspect my connection with him," Max said, anxiously.

"Muntener may have talked?"

"I think that's highly unlikely," the younger man said. "Erik stands to lose a great deal if he informs on us. I happen to know that his student finances are rather precarious."

Ziegler's face clouded. He refilled his cup from the small china pot, added a measured amount of cream, and said:

"Mason's somehow connected you with the books, old chap. Evidently, he was hoping the local police would find incriminating evidence at your apartment. Now how could he possibly have latched on to you?"

Max Fifield averted his gaze from the critical regard of the Swiss, sipped his coffee nervously and glanced through the tall windows at the trams sliding into Belle Vue.

"That, I'm afraid," he replied, after a while, "is a complete mystery to me."

"I told you Special Branch were as keen as mustard," Ziegler said, taking a perverse sort of satisfaction in this validation of his views. "George Mason, by Jove! He's on to us. I knew he'd be trouble the moment he strolled into my shop the other day and started looking up historical architecture. How would a gumshoe like him normally be interested in works by Palladio and the like?"

The salesman quietly sipped his drink, letting the rhetorical question pass. His companion took up the tabloid again, ostensibly to finish the crossword puzzle, humming half-aloud a popular Swiss melody. After a while, he said:

"We'll fix George Mason once and for all. There's very little chance he'll locate the missing books. They're in a very secure place and Hugh Rokeby's arriving any day now from Philadelphia to take them out of the country for good. We don't know for certain how much Mason knows. But just to make absolutely sure he can't interfere at this critical stage of the agenda, we'll set up an elaborate decoy system."

Max Fifield gave a deep sigh of relief. He was out from under Ziegler's critical gaze, and it seemed to him almost as if the Swiss relished the prospect of jousting with the English investigator, as if he had an old score to settle with him, though he had never intimated what that might be.

"I was pretty sure you'd come up with something," he said, approvingly. "I take it we shall have no further problems with regard to Inspector George Mason?"

"You have my word on it," Ziegler assured him, with his customary panache. "Now, if you'll excuse me, my dear

Max, I must get back to my little business. There's an important Japanese client coming at eleven."

"Architecture?" quizzed the salesman, humorously.

"Actually no," returned the Swiss. "Interestingly enough, he collects books and shipping records on whaling, particularly out of the old New England ports. I've a signed copy of *Moby Dick* he's bound to go for. Just a question of striking a price."

The Japanese are certainly into whaling, Max thought, but did not comment.

chapter 13

MONDAY DAWNED BRIGHTLY south of the alps. Count Flavio de Montesedina was sitting after lunch on the shaded terrace of his villa with his wife Amelia, before setting off for Stresa Station. They were watching the yachts clustering round Isola Bella for the start of the afternoon regatta, while enjoying a glass of his flowery estate wine.

"How long do you expect to be gone?" Amelia enquired, alluding to his departure that afternoon for the capital.

"About two weeks," the count said, "at the very minimum. Will you be bored?"

"Emphatically not," Amelia replied. "Tomorrow, I shall go to Biasca to stay with my sister for a week. When I return, I shall have plenty to do getting my paintings ready for the Milan Biennale."

Flavio sipped his wine thoughtfully.

"Do you think you'll have more success this year?" he asked. "Your views of the lake, especially the ones with yachts or wading birds, are most impressive."

"I'm glad that you at least have faith in my work," Amelia said, reaching across the table to pat his arm affectionately. "As for the judges, who can tell?"

"The problem today," her husband remarked, "is that there are no longer any objective standards for judging works of art. No aesthetic values, as there were in former times, when academies and salons established recognized criteria."

"What you are saying, in effect," his wife added, "is that standards have become increasingly subjective. If someone comes along and claims he has created a work of art, or of music, he expects to be taken at his word."

"And very often is," quipped the count. "Look what passes for modern art nowadays. Frankly, it's risible."

Amelia rose and walked to the edge of the terrace to dead-head some nasturtiums.

"At least," she remarked, turning back to him, "the adjudicators this year are fairly conservative. Old Professore Luzi from Turin, for one."

"Then you're definitely in with a chance. I happen to know that Luzi is very fond of landscape painting. He's one of the old school, who's been lecturing on art history and appreciation since the year dot."

"Let's hope you're right," Amelia said, laughingly.

"In any event," Flavio continued, "after July 10th, when the coup will have taken place and a new regime established, I'll recommend you for Minister of the Arts."

Amelia returned to the table, sat down again and looked earnestly at her husband.

"You are quite sure of what you are about to do?" she asked. "There won't be any last-minute hitches, will there? Nothing that can go wrong?"

"The Amadeo Agenda is far too advanced now," he assured her, "for any mishap to occur. General Granelli has already moved his brigade, the 5th Light Infantry, to the Rome area. All necessary funding has been secured. Final preparations will be put in hand during the coming week."

"Even so," his wife said, "I have my misgivings. There's bound to be a large element of risk in an enterprise of this type."

The distinguished aristocrat rose to his feet and grasped her hands reassuringly.

"The main element is surprise," he said. "Nobody outside our small inner circle has the faintest inkling of our objectives. Least of all the government."

" I do hope you're right," she said, "for both our sakes."

Flavio smiled his rather suave smile and released her hands. Glancing at his watch, he said: "It's almost time to go. Why don't I fetch my valise from the bedroom, while you bring the sedan round to the front drive?"

"Will do," agreed Amelia, half reconciled to whatever the future held and suppressing her innermost feelings.

Minutes later, they were on their way to the railway station. Amelia dropped him off by the entrance and headed straight to her studio, not far from the villa. In her rear-view mirror she watched her husband, clad in a pale-beige two-piece suit and clutching a large valise, stride purposefully into the building. She had some finishing touches to add to two of her entries in the Biennale, after which she would take an early dinner alone and spend the rest of the evening making preparations for tomorrow's trip by train to Biasca, a country town in Ticino, due north of Bellinzona. Her sister Renata, who had affairs to attend to in Locarno, would meet her there for lunch and accompany her on the last leg of the journey. Amelia was looking forward to it, not having visited her sister in almost a year.

Count Flavio waited a few moments on the platfrom for the arrival of the *Monteverdi*, the crack Geneva-Milano express, hoping there would be a spare seat on one of the busiest services in the region. He was in luck. A handful of tourists alighted when it pulled into Stresa, leaving two va-

164

cant seats in the first-class compartment. He occupied the one nearest the window and took out the copy of *Corriere della Sera* he had bought at the station kiosk, to catch up on the latest national and international news. There were the usual problems, the chief of which being the shortfall in the budget and the endless debates about cuts in services. The numerous socialist parties would fight tooth and nail against any proposals by the center-right government to trim back spending on education, health care, pensions and the like. Let them do their worst, he mused, in what small amount of time was left to them. Under the new regime he was helping to inaugurate, left-wing and liberal parties would be completely irrelevant. All public services would be adequately financed by innovative fiscal measures to be put into effect at the earliest possible opportunity. Professore Ilona Rosso, in consultation with a university colleague sympathetic to their cause who was expert in public finance, would brief him that very day on the details. He folded his newspaper and relaxed, taking in the views of the southern reaches of Lake Maggiore as the express sped towards Arona, the last scheduled stop before Milan.

The lady professor was waiting for him at the station buffet when his train reached its destination. With fifty minutes to kill before his connection to Rome, he bought a herbal tea at the service counter and joined her as she was finishing her light refreshment.

Ilona Rosso greeted him warmly, eyed his large valise and remarked:

"You're here for the long haul, aren't you?"

"It's my wife, Amelia," he explained, humorously. "She always takes good care of my needs, simple as they are."

"Not all that simple," Ilona quipped, "from the look of things."

Flavio sipped his tea, glad of some liquid refreshment after the train journey, and appraised his fellow conspirator. She was a well-built woman in early middle age, whose short hair was prematurely gray. Her strong, almost masculine features struck him as somehow more attractive than he recalled from their first encounter at Lugano, though he was at pains to see exactly why. Perhaps it was her dark, intense eyes and rather sensuous mouth, he eventually decided, soon averting his gaze to avoid the impression of staring.

"You were going to brief me on public finance," he ventured.

The professor glanced round, to make sure they were not overheard from the nearby tables. In subdued tones, she said:

"I've gone over things in general terms with my colleague, Professore Fausto Valentini. The finer details can be worked out later, once we are established in power."

"It must be done in such a way as to mollify the Italian public," the count emphasized.

"It shall be," Ilona announced, confidently. "The main sop to the public will be a fifty per cent cut in income tax."

"And how will the balance be made up?" Flavio enquired, whose feelings of skepticism were tinged with sneaking admiration of the boldness of her proposal.

"There are two principal measures," she explained, "both of which are revolutionary and will radically improve public finances."

"And they are?"

"First, we shall expand the National Lottery, which already brings in a considerable amount of money, by tripling the prize kitty. Then we shall introduce a special tax on Internet gambling."

"You will meet strong opposition from the Church," the count cautioned, "on the grounds of public morality."

Ilona Rosso smiled blandly back at him.

"You know as well as I do, my dear fellow," she countered, "that such protests will have little practical effect, especially since the new regime will be far more supportive of church positions on social questions than any administration in living memory. Consider the recent tussles between church and state over bioethics, for example."

"Stem cell research, for example? In-vitro fertilization?"

"To name just two contentious issues. When the bishops realize that we are largely in agreement with them, they'll soon tone down their objections to gambling."

"They'll register their protest and leave it at that," Flavio agreed. "But what makes you think a tax on Internet gambling will bridge the gap?"

"Have you any idea, my dear sir," Ilona replied, archly, "how much is spent on on-line poker alone?"

The count shook his head. It was not something he had much considered until now, being only vaguely aware of the phenomenon from occasional coverage in the press.

"It runs over a billion euros per annum," the professor informed him. "A veritable goldmine for public finances."

"That will be trillions in lire," Flavio put in, with a glow of satisfaction, "once we reinstate our national currency."

"Think of all the programs we can introduce with that kind of money," Ilona said. "We'll have the public eating out of our hands."

Sitting back to finish his tea and inwardly marveling at how well the lady professor had thought things through, a glance at his watch told him it was time to make for the train.

"You ready?" he asked. "The Rome express leaves in about ten minutes. We must be sure of obtaining seats."

"You go on ahead," Ilona said, "while I collect my suitcases from the lockers on the lower level."

"Suitcases?" quipped the count. "You have more than one?"

"For the long haul," she replied, with a sly smile, as they left the buffet.

⇥⇤

George Mason lingered over breakfast that morning, waiting for the mail to arrive. He opened Friday's copy of *Tages Anzeiger* that the head waiter had saved for him at his request, to read again the curious item that had so arrested his attention on the Announcements page that day. The For Sale column was next to the Personal column. Out of curiosity, he scanned the entries by unattached men and women seeking relationships. The main quality sought by the females was *gepflegt,* which his pocket dictionary informed him meant 'refined', 'cultured' or even 'sophisticated'. Swiss nationality was also a must. They evidently didn't want much truck with foreigners, he considered, as he measured himself mentally against the list of other requirements. The males, on the other hand, stressed appearance and character as the most desirable qualities, making few references to nationality. Perhaps they were more open-minded in that respect, which was good news for the scores of young Asian women he had noticed on the city streets. From the extent of such advertisements, which appeared on a daily basis, the Zurich broadsheet appeared to be a significant marriage bureau catering to a surprisingly large number of singles for a city of this modest size.

He soon switched his attention back to the For Sale column. At the head was a most intriguing entry. It read: 'First editions of rare books by Palladio, Ackerman, Hemingway and others. Prices by negotiation. Box No. ZXJ 957'. Could this be the breakthrough he was looking for, he had asked himself? The fence who had received the stolen items would have to unload them at some point, and an advertisement in this widely-read daily might be as discreet a way as any, since the seller could carefully vet the responders before revealing his own identity. A rather clever tactic, he mused; but not quite clever enough. The vendor would be assuming that, with the passage of time, any investigations by the local police would have been shelved in favor of more pressing matters. But he was overlooking one key fact that he could not possibly be aware of. Scotland Yard Special Branch was now very much involved. This was no cold case.

He requested fresh coffee as the dining-room gradually cleared of late arrivals for the buffet breakfast and reviewed his own strategy. Aware that Chief Inspector Harrington was breathing down his neck, and that he had barely a week left before his recall to London, he had penned a reply to the box number, representing himself as an English collector of antiquities, including rare books. He had used hotel notepaper, which included an address and telephone number; but he doubted that the advertiser would ring. He thought it much more likely that he would, in the first instance, respond in writing. Since he had taken his reply by hand to the editorial offices of *Tages Anzeiger* late on Friday afternoon, today was the earliest date he could expect a response. He was the last person left at table when the postman duly arrived.

"Herr Mason," said the young receptionist, entering from the lobby ten minutes later to hand him a small envelope. "*Ein Brief.*"

The detective accepted it a little warily, surprised but quite pleased that a reply had come so soon. He examined it carefully before opening it. It was the finest quality stationery, but did not carry a Zurich postmark. It had been posted on Saturday in Sorenberg, wherever that was. Slitting it cleanly with his table-knife, he read the following contents, written in English in deference no doubt to his nationality:

'Many thanks for your reply, one of several. Regret that, owing to business commitments, am unable to be in Zurich at this time to negotiate. Giving you first refusal on my tradables, because I dealt successfully with English buyers in the past. Please make arrangements to visit Sorenberg as soon as convenient. Instructions on arrival will be waiting for you *poste restante* at Sorenberg Postamt. Sincerely – Hermann Gertler.'

Mason refolded the missive and placed it back in the grained, ivory-tinted envelope, with a strong feeling that his luck was in. The vendor obviously felt safer dealing with a foreign buyer, with someone less likely to know the provenance of the stolen titles. Hermann Gertler, he mused. Who precisely was this new player in this absorbing game? A contact of Anton Ziegler's, perhaps? Rolf Kubler may have background on him, but there was no time to consult the canny lieutenant, who was away until Wednesday on a residential course at Airolo. He would have to proceed alone, find out where Sorenberg was and get there without delay. Today seemed as good a day as any, since time was running out and there were few enough promising leads. Interpol were looking into Laszlo Polke's financial affairs, but had not so far reported back; and the Carabinieri had barely begun their enquiries along the shores of Lake Maggiore. Unsure how far he would have to travel, he returned to his room, brushed his teeth and packed a small valise in the event of an overnight stay.

By mid-morning, he was heading along the Lim-matquai on his way to the Hauptbahnhof. Once there, he bought a copy of the London *Times* to read on the train and then went straight to the information desk to enquire how to reach Sorenberg. The clerk explained to him that he should first take the local train to Lucerne, which ran at hourly intervals. At Lucerne, he should transfer to the Bern express. The small alpine settlement of Sorenberg, she explained, lay beneath the Brienzer Rothorn, one of the higher peaks in the northern alps. He should alight at Giswil, in a region known locally as the Emmental Forest, and from there take the post-bus up the steep valley. Mason thanked her, feeling relieved that he was not in for too long a journey and at the same time intrigued at the curious name she had mentioned. Emmentaler, he knew, was a famous Swiss cheese; the one with the holes. Did it really grow on trees, he wondered humorously?

He joined the short queue at the booking-office and bought a day-return ticket, fully expecting to be back in Zurich by nightfall. Consulting the train indicator, he found that he had only ten minutes to wait before the next departure at eleven o'clock. He hurried along the platform to make sure of obtaining a seat and was soon comfortably ensconced in a second-class compartment, reviewing the news from England. *The Times* airmail edition arrived here a day late, so that it yesterday's news he was reading. That did not trouble the detective, whose main interest was in cricket and in the Fourth Test Match between England and India. David Gower, he noted with satisfaction, had scored a century in his usual fluent style, to put the home side in a commanding position. How would that young Yorkshire seam bowler perform in his maiden test, he wondered, when England took the field? Since it was a five-day match, there would be time later in the week to catch up on the details.

The stopping train called at all the upmarket suburban settlements on the south side of the lake, before picking up speed through the Zurich Oberland on its way to Zug, the last stop before Lucerne. His observant eye took in the features of the landscape, the rolling hills, broad copses, farms and orchards, the quaint half-timbered dwellings. The town of Zug lay beside a large lake dotted with yachts, against a backdrop of snow-capped alps that seemed to have moved measurably nearer. Which one of them was the Brienzer Rothorn, he wondered, marveling that hundreds of peaks could each have an individual name and characteristics well-known to those who lived close to them. For centuries, the Swiss had lived in fear and awe of the high mountains, while grazing their cattle on the lower slopes. That these same slopes had become a winter playground for many in more recent decades was due, he had read somewhere, to his fellow-countrymen, to those young aristocrats with ample leisure who had introduced skiing. The herdsmen must have been truly amazed on first seeing these English eccentrics slide down steep slopes on thin slats of wood. But they soon cottoned on to the economic potential, supplementing their farm incomes by doubling as ski instructors.

Leaving the train at Lucerne and consulting the indicator, he discovered that he had just missed a connection to Bern. Thankful that Swiss train frequencies were almost always hourly, he deposited his valise in the left-luggage lockers and strolled out into the midday sunshine to watch the large paddle-boats like the *William Tell* load up with passengers. He was reminded of his earlier visit to Rutli Meadow, the birthplace of the Swiss Federation. It was now the height of the summer season, with tourists milling about the older parts of the city, with its open-air markets and the famous covered bridge spanning the swift-flowing river just before it emptied into the lake. Gauging his available time carefully, he decided to explore for himself, marveling at the hand-painted scenes from Swiss country life that covered the ceiling the entire length of the sturdy wooden structure. At the opposite end, he discovered a cobbled riverside walk heavily shaded with trees whose branches drooped close to the water, where tables from a series of restaurants were invitingly placed. Much as he would have liked to spend an hour or so in such an attractive spot, time did not permit. He lingered for a while to absorb the atmosphere, then retraced his steps to the railway station.

In just under two hours he alighted at Giswil, feeling rather surprised that a mainline express should stop at such a quiet-seeming village. Yet stop it did, almost momentarily, allowing him just sufficient time to scramble out onto the deserted platfrom with his luggage. He watched the train disappear down the line and made for the bus-stop just outside the station. The region was served by the post-bus, which delivered the mail while ferrying passengers to the remoter settlements. He consulted the *Fahrplan* for several minutes, finding that service times differed according to the days of the week. Mondays, unfortunately, had a restricted service to Sorenberg. As far as he could make out, the next bus was due at 3.55 p.m. He checked his watch; it was just turned three, involving him in another longish wait. Glancing down the deserted main street, practically the only street in Giswil, he espied no sidewalk tables where he could have relaxed over a drink. But it was an agreeable enough little place, the terrain rising steeply beyond it through sloping meadows to a broad swath of spruce forest below the starker, treeless slopes with snowy peaks. Feeling that he was now truly in the alps, he sat down in the shade, lit one of his small Dutch cigars and prepared to wait, sincerely hoping that he had read the timetable correctly.

He need not have been concerned. At exactly 3.45 p.m. the yellow post-bus arrived. The driver-mailman jumped clear, went straight to the rear of the vehicle and took out a large leather satchel, which he deposited at the adjacent post office. He stretched his legs for a while, relit a half-smoked cigarette and glanced curiously at George Mason.

"Sorenberg?" he enquired, eventually.

The detective nodded and stepped forward, as the driver remounted and turned on the ignition.

"*Einfach?*" he asked.

"*Hin und zuruck.*" Mason thought it best to buy a return ticket.

"*Drei Franken, zwanzig pfennig.*"

The detective counted out his small change and gave three francs, twenty pennies in exchange for a ticket. As he clambered aboard and occupied a front seat, he felt quite pleased at his brief exchange in German. It was part of the appeal of country places, in contrast to the cities, that the locals rarely spoke English. He sat back to enjoy the ride, as the bus wound steadily up the snaking roads, past green meadows with grazing cattle and through the forest, with its steep waterfalls and rushing streams.

It was in places quite a hair-raising ride, with steep drops at blind bends the driver negotiated with a verve that unnerved George Mason. While fully appreciating the scenery, he felt a keen sense of relief when the post-bus pulled up sharp right outside Sorenberg Postamt after the forty-minute drive. Mason climbed down and watched with creeping dismay as the driver collected another leather satchel from the rear, unlocked the night safe in the wall of the post office and deposited the mail there. As he drove off, heading even higher up the pass, the detective approached the main entrance to the building. His luck was out; it had closed at four o'clock. He felt a moment of panic.

Rural business hours were in force, the postmistress having evidently already left to prepare her herder-husband's dinner and feed her goats and chickens. There was no way he was going to retrieve Gertler's letter *poste restante* that day. He looked around him in some anxiety, his eye following the line of the village street before glancing upwards at the sharp horn-like peak that dominated the skyline. The Brienzer Rothorn, no less, he decided. A small group of people sat over drinks at an outdoor café fifty yards away. Apart from them, there was no discernable human presence.

He grabbed his valise and began walking back the way he had come, having noticed a sports hotel of the type used by skiers and hikers at the foot of the village. The objective now was to locate Hermann Gertler in person, but he could not do that until he had booked accommodation. The Hotel Edelweiss looked well within his budget, catering as it did for outdoor types. He reached it after a few minutes' walk and enquired at Reception. The clerk informed him that they had a single room without bath available at a modest tariff that included a buffet breakfast. To Mason's pique, no evening meals were served, which meant that he would have to look elsewhere, perhaps find an inn farther up the village, unless his luck was in and Herr Gertler invited him to dinner. Accepting the room-key and mounting the short flight of wooden stairs to the mezzanine floor, he wondered if he was being realistic. Why a *poste restante* letter, after all? If Gertler lived in the village, wouldn't he surely have met him in person? Perhaps he was merely being extra-cautious, as befitted a dealer in stolen goods, and was proceeding slowly, by carefully-planned steps.

Once inside his small room, which contained a divan bed, simple pinewood furniture, a wash-basin and mirror, he put down his valise and leafed through the phone-book, which covered Giswil, Sorenberg and neighboring settlements whose names meant little to him. Under G, he found Gerthoffer, Gertmann and Gertwil; but no Gertlers of any description. He replaced the phone-book on the rickety night table, crossed to the window and looked out at the towering peaks that seemed to glower over the village. The explanation was simple, he decided. Gertler's number was ex-Directory, as one might expect of a person in his profession. He would freshen up quickly and call at Reception on his way out. They should know everyone's address in such a small village.

The clerk at the desk, however, looked puzzled.

"Hermann Gertler?" she enquired. "I know of no one by that name. But be kind to wait one moment, while I ask the manager. He has lived here nearly all his life."

Mason waited, expectantly. After a short while the young woman returned, accompanied by the manager, a fit-looking gentleman in hiking gear.

"There is a family Gertler living in Langnau," he said. "But I have not met Hermann Gertler. Perhaps he moved away, to Zurich or Bern, as many villagers from these parts do, and has only recently returned to the area."

That seemed to George Mason quite plausible, if beside the point.

"How far away is Langnau?" he enquired.

"About thirty kilometers. You must take the train from Giswil, but there is no bus from here until tomorrow morning. Six o'clock sharp, from the Postamt."

"In that case, I'll wait until tomorrow," the detective said. "Herr Gertler is supposed to show up here in Sorenberg, by prior arrangement."

"Very well," returned the other. "Is your room to your satisfaction?"

"Quite adequate," replied Mason, more out of politeness than conviction. "Since you don't serve dinner, perhaps…."

The manager cut him short.

"Try Der Rothorn, an inn at the far end of the village," he said. "They serve evening meals from six o'clock on. They close at ten."

Mason thanked him on his way out, deciding to make the most of his short stay in such bracing surroundings by getting some overdue exercise in the mountain air. He took the road up through the village, crossed a footbridge over a crystal-clear mountain spring and discovered a path signposted 'Brienzer Rothorn'. He followed it doggedly as it zigzagged upwards past small farms where a few alpine cattle grazed, until he had climbed well beyond the habitation line. The peak still loomed far above him when he realized he was tiring. Sitting down on a tree stump, he caught his breath while taking in the magnificent scenery. It would be a place to bring his wife Adele on a short vacation; she especially liked lakes and mountains, hence their planned autumn trip to Cumbria.

The inn named for the majestic peak was open by the time he reached it. He stooped beneath the low lintel to enter a large dining-room with bare pinewood tables. Groups of locals sat with steins of beer, playing a game similar to dominoes. They paid him scant attention as he took a seat and scanned the menu, opting for the restaurant special called, unsurprisingly, the *Emmentaler*. As he waited patiently, almost interminably it seemed, for the waitress to reappear with his order, he overheard snatches of conversation from the gaming tables. It did not sound much like German as he knew it, recalling something Kubler had told him, that this was an entirely separate language that had developed in isolation over many centuries, owing to Switzerland's natural boundaries. Listening to these rude herdsmen without understanding a word, he could well believe it.

His meal eventually arrived in a plain earthenware bowl, accompanied by a stein of the local ale. His long climb and the fact that he had skipped lunch had sharpened his appetite. Allowing the bowl to cool for a few moments while he sampled his beer, he soon tackled it, discovering a most palatable dish of chopped pork and leeks layered with pasta and smothered in a thick cheese sauce whose tangy flavor spoke of Emmental. There were definite perks to an assignment of this nature, he mused, sitting at length in contentment over a jug of fresh coffee to round off a satisfying meal, while enjoying accordion music and yodeling from the radio, the clattering of domino chips on bare wood and the guttural sound of Swiss-German.

He slept quite late the following morning, from his exertions of the previous day. Climbing alpine paths had obviously taken more out of him than he had anticipated. Easing his limbs off the simple bed, he washed and dressed quickly and went down to the dining-room, only to discover that breakfast service in this sports hotel had ended at eight-thirty, catering no doubt to early risers who would be hiking up the Rothorn to watch the sunrise, or some such energetic pursuit. Cursing his luck, he returned to his room, packed his valise and checked out, heading straight to the Postamt to collect Gertler's letter. In need of a coffee to help him think, he repaired to the sidewalk café a short distance away along the main street, sat down and examined the postmark. The letter, curiously, had been mailed in Bern, where he recalled Max Fifield's head office was located. Was that mere coincidence, he wondered, slitting the envelope open?

The contents of the letter were not what he had been anticipating, and it was several minutes before he fully absorbed the implications. It read: *Profuse regrets at not being here to greet you. Called away at short notice to conclude a deal at Locarno. If still interested in my inventory, make your way there tomorrow, Tuesday. Check into Hotel Spitz and order dinner. I shall join you there later.—*

Yours, H. Gertler

The detective sat back, wondering what to make of it all. He re-read the message. A trip to Locarno right now would certainly be an inconvenience, Gertler was right about that. But the message seemed genuine enough on the face of it, especially since it was being left to him to decide whether to pursue the matter further or not. The Swiss most likely had other parties interested in what he euphemistically described as his 'inventory'. And what other options did he, George Mason, have at this stage, with time fast running out? He finished his coffee philosophically, as the mountain village began slowly to come to life, centered mainly on the post office and the small general store attached to it. He had now to figure out how to reach Locarno, deciding that his best bet, since he had a return ticket, would be to retrace his outward journey as far as Lucerne and enquire at the information desk there. Grasping his valise, he strolled back to the Postamt, checked the schedule of the post-bus to Giswil and waited patiently for it to arrive. Twenty-five minutes later, he was on his way back down the steep alpine valley.

chapter 14

HUGH ROKEBY ALIGHTED from his American Airways overnight flight from Philadelphia to Geneva's Cointrin Airport at 10.20 a.m. on Tuesday, July 6th. In a confident frame of mind, he caught the rail link for the short ride into the city, arriving there just after eleven. A long-established dealer in rare books, prints and maps, he was looking forward to doing good business with a certain Anton Ziegler, who was coming down from Zurich to meet him. He went directly to the men's room to freshen up after intermittent sleep on the airliner, then repaired to Starbuck's on the main concourse for coffee and croissants, while awaiting his contact. Ziegler had a most interesting book inventory. But how dependable was he? He was well-known internationally in antiquarian circles, yet some of the trade that crossed national boundaries was of questionable provenance. One could rarely be one hundred per cent sure on matters of authenticity; that was one of the risks of his profession, a calculated risk that he was prepared to take. So far, it had served him well, earning him a solid bank of clients on the East Coast, mainly private individuals whose collections rarely came under public scrutiny, except in ad hoc tax investigations by the Internal Revenue Service.

He could charge double the sum he was paying the Swiss for first editions of works by the likes of Palladio and Ackerman, if somewhat less for modern authors such as Hemingway. And a hitherto unknown piano score by Mozart was indeed priceless. As the minutes passed and his elegant pocket-watch registered eleven-thirty, he began to wonder if something had happened to delay his contact, scanning the busy pedestrian traffic on the station concourse for signs of an elderly gentleman with a goatee beard. That was how Anton Ziegler had described himself, as an aid to recognition, in the course of their last telephone conversation. His eye was caught momentarily by a guitarist dressed as a medieval troubadour entertaining passengers in the lounge area close to the platforms. That was one of the beauties of European travel, he reflected; there was always something completely unexpected, something they could pull back across centuries of national culture.

"Good morning, Herr Rokeby," came a voice to his rear, wresting him from his brief reverie.

The American turned in pleasant surprise, recognizing at once the Zurich-based dealer. He sprang up to greet him.

"Had a good flight?" Ziegler enquired, as they both sat down.

"So-so," replied Rokeby. "You know how it is on these overnight trips."

"I can well imagine," the Swiss said, "even though I have never flown the Atlantic."

"You've never been to the States?" queried the American, in surprise.

"Only once, some years ago. On the QE2, to visit a book fair in Boston."

181

"A fine city," the other said. "I do good business there and my daughter attends the university, majoring in Art History."

"If you've finished your coffee," Ziegler said, unconcerned about his family background, "we have a train to catch. I already bought both our tickets, to save time."

"Very thoughtful of you," the buyer remarked, draining his cup and grasping a small leather suitcase. "Lead on, by all means. I'm entirely in your hands."

The Swiss headed at a brisk pace in the direction of Platform 3, where they were just in time to catch a northbound train. As it pulled out of the station and picked up speed along the shores of Lac Leman, the American was much captivated by the scenery, looking down from the compartment window over the red-tiled rooftops of the outer suburbs at the yachts tacking across the broad expanse of water.

"How is business in the States?" Ziegler asked, eventually.

"Fairly steady," Rokeby replied. "One of the most successful lines, really an evergreen, is books on Americana. Particularly those dealing with the opening up of the West. Can't get enough of them to meet the demand."

"What about European items?" the other prompted.

"They're for the more sophisticated, wealthier collector, mainly living in the East. Wall Street brokers, fund managers, corporate CEOs and the like. They're also in the market for paintings, sculptures, antiques. Anything that is more or less guaranteed to appreciate in value, to preserve and increase their assets."

"More dependable than stock markets, eh?" Ziegler asked, with heavy irony.

"You bet," Rokeby stressed. "When do I get to see your inventory?"

"You have a ready market for it?" the Swiss enquired.

"Practically sold already," Rokeby said. "I've mentioned them to several serious collectors in Philadelphia, New York and Baltimore. They are *very* interested."

"I understand from your phone-call that you also have business in Brig?"

"It'll take just a couple of hours," the American said. "A dealer there is offering some military diaries from our Civil War period. I've arranged to meet him at two o'clock."

"You'll be in good time," Ziegler assured him. "Brig is the next stop after Martigny, which we should reach in just over an hour. When you have concluded your deal, we shall proceed to Locarno, where I have a small personal matter to attend to. I've booked us both in at Hotel Mirafiori on the lake-front, for an overnight stay."

"I thought your premises were in Zurich?" Rokeby asked, in some surprise.

Anton Ziegler averted his gaze from the searching eyes of the buyer.

"Part of my stock is temporarily housed elsewhere," he explained, evasively. "For practical reasons."

Hugh Rokeby thought he caught the drift of the other's remark, but he didn't press the matter. Business was business; it was as simple as that. What the Swiss antiquarian was offering him was just too good to pass up.

"Locarno sounds fine by me," he said. "Isn't it by one of the large Italian lakes?"

"Just across the border with Italy," the Swiss explained, "at the northern end of Lago di Maggiore. A very scenic area."

"I'd like to do a spot of sight-seeing, if we have time," the other said.

"We shall make time tomorrow morning," Ziegler assured him, "so that you can take full advantage of your short stay in Switzerland."

"You have a wonderful little country here," the American said, appreciatively. "You *are* part of the European Union, aren't you? Tell me if I'm wrong. My wife, whose maternal ancestry derives from Freiburg in the Jura Mountains, particularly wanted to know."

Anton Ziegler returned a smile heavy with irony, that his visitor should ask such a question at this critical juncture. At the same time, he felt an inner glow. The very presence of this American virtually guaranteed the success of Amadeo. Not even that flatfoot George Mason could intervene now.

"The Swiss are an independent-minded people," he explained. "There is no way we would dilute our national sovereignty in something rapidly approaching a United States of Europe. No way at all, my dear sir. We Swiss have lived too long in our alpine fortress for ambitions like that. We are bankers to the world and will survive very nicely that way, as also on lucrative trading pacts with our European neighbors."

"That was my impression," Rokeby said. "My wife was not so sure."

"When you get back to the States," Ziegler went on, in conspiratorial vein, "tell her that radical changes are about to take place in Europe, events that will shake the EU to its foundations. And not in the distant future either."

Hugh Rokeby regarded him curiously, wondering if the Swiss antiquarian was merely indulging in hyperbole and anti-integration sentiment. But in so far as he could tell Anton Ziegler seemed, incredibly, to be in deadly earnest. His wife Freni would be most intrigued when he reported back to her, on arrival at their custom-built home overlook-

ing the Schuylkill River in an up-market district of Philadelphia.

⧆

George Mason reached Lucerne just after midday, after catching the Bern-Lucerne express at Giswil. The clerk
at the information desk gave him two alternative routes
to Locarno and, since there was no rush to arrive before
evening, he chose the less direct and more scenic. He first
caught the service leading over the Brunig Pass to the town
of Brienz, marveling at how a passenger train of a dozen
coaches, assisted by an extra cog-rail, could inch its way
down the steep far side of the pass, at what he estimated
to be a speed of less than ten miles per hour. A marvel of
railway engineering, he reflected, as he alighted at Brienz,
which his rudimentary geography told him was on the other side of the famed Brienzer Rothorn he had viewed last
evening from Sorenberg, and which he had made a determined effort to ascend part-way on foot.

Brienz lay at the foot of the pass and at the eastern end
of the Brienzersee. Its main industry seemed to be the man-
ufacture of cuckoo clocks in all shapes and sizes. It crossed
his mind to buy one as a surprise gift to Chief Inspector
Harrington, just to see his reaction; but he dismissed the
idea, having already overrun his budget. A large passenger
vessel, *Der Schwan*, was moored to a long jetty sporting a
booking-office, ice-cream vendors and a waiting-room with
the necessary services. He paid a quick visit to the restroom,
before joining the long queue of tourists, mainly retirees
anticipating a relaxing cruise down to Interlaken, so-named
for its position between the Brienzersee and the Thunersee to the west. The live onboard commentary pointed out
items of interest on the way, mainly famous peaks such as

the Eiger and the Matterhorn lying to the south in the massive central section of the alps. Mason was intrigued, the more so since the ship had a spacious, oak-paneled restaurant serving warm dishes and very palatable bottled ales. Having skipped breakfast in order not to miss the post-bus from Sorenberg, he was quite hungry by early afternoon, treating himself to a Wienerschnitzel with French fries and an endive salad.

He could certainly take to a life like this, he mused, regarding with a degree of envy the ship's crew, who got to spend their working hours every day among such splendid scenery. But was it all sunshine and roses? Weren't there times when the weather was bad, the sky overcast and the surface turbulent? Had there been shipwrecks even? It seemed to him quite possible on a lake this size, open to everything the elements could hurl at it. Mountain storms were in a class of their own. The winds would experience a funneling effect from the nature of the landscape, redoubling their strength. The sober thought tempered his envy and he was in a contented frame of mind by the time they berthed at Interlaken. He could almost have thanked Hermann Gertler for giving him this opportunity to see more of Switzerland than he had anticipated. Perhaps he would indeed thank him when they met that evening over dinner at Hotel Spitz.

Interlaken struck him as a tourist trap, with long rows of shops and boutiques selling mainly souvenirs, interspersed with Swiss and Italian restaurants. It was also milling with tourists and he felt glad to be on his way again as his connecting train pulled out of the station and headed west along the shore of the Thunersee, before veering south towards the Loetschberg Tunnel. Brig was the first major stop beyond that. Out of the corner of his eye, he glimpsed an elderly gentleman with a goatee beard, accompanied by a tall, smartly-dressed individual, disappearing into the station buffet. Turning his head fully, he was just too late for a better look, dismissing the thought that he had just espied a certain antiquarian book-dealer well-known to him. Anton Ziegler would after all, he considered, hardly be the only man in Switzerland sporting a goatee. Besides, didn't he have a business to run in Zurich?

A bit farther down the line, he alighted at Domodossola for his connection to Locarno, noting with interest that he was now in Ticino, the Italian-speaking province bordering Lakes Lugano and Maggiore. He was reminded somehow of skiing trips he had made to the Dolomites in years past, with his wife Adele. There was un unmistakable Italian ambience even here, a sensation of warmth and friendliness not solely deriving from the softer climate south of the alps. There were vineyards too, always a welcome sight to Mason's eyes, covering the slopes between the towns and villages. He would request a local vintage with his evening meal, he decided, as the stopping train made steady if unhurried progress on the last leg of his absorbing journey. On arrival at Locarno, he soon located Hotel Spitz in the main shopping center, about fifty yards from the railway station. He booked a room for the night, as instructed, and found he had ample time to explore the elegant lakeside city before dinner.

Hotel Spitz was a modest establishment catering to the less affluent tourist and middle-ranking Swiss officials and businessmen who had affairs to attend to in Locarno. It was a far cry from the luxury hotels with extensive gardens terraced down to the lake. But it suited Mason's budget. His room was rather cramped, a private bathroom having been added at a later stage, at the expense of the original room dimensions. It was comfortably fitted out, with a television set and a mini-bar, but the windows overlooked the backs of office buildings and the railway track. Mason remained there just long enough to watch the evening news and take a shower, before going down to the dining-room in a mood of keen anticipation, feeling that now at last, after all his groundwork, he was about to make a break-through in the case.

The dining-room was half-full when he was shown to a table for two that overlooked a quiet side-street and handed a menu printed in Italian and German, which he pondered for several minutes. The names of the dishes were not as familiar to him as those in the Zurich eateries, except for an item near the bottom of the list. *Forelle gebacken*, he decided, could only be locally caught trout. It came with wild rice and mushrooms and would go well with a white wine. He placed the order with the waiter, to include a half-carafe of Riesling from the Valais, all the local wines being reds. The waiter looked questioningly at the vacant seat opposite him and the detective explained, in his best German, that he would be joined later. Left to himself, he glanced round the room to weigh up his fellow-diners, feeling a vicarious companionship with them. Those at the table nearest him, a young Italian couple, perhaps even newly-weds, smiled and bade him a *buona sera,* a greeting he returned.

Service was slow. By the time his food appeared, he had already sipped half his wine, much appreciating its cool tang on a warm evening. Since the trout was served whole, he patiently set about filleting it, pleased to discover at his first sampling that it had been stuffed with herbs that enhanced the flavor. Trout, in his experience, generally had a rather bland taste, but this was classic Italian cuisine. The mushrooms, of the large Portabello variety, were delicious. The couple nearby, having marked him for an Englishman, seemed eager to start a conversation. Uncharacteristically, he did not respond; he had too much on his mind. He had almost finished his meal when the waiter approached.

"A Herr Gertler telephoned, with a message for you," he said.

Mason glanced up, expectantly.

"And?" he asked.

"He presents his compliments, but he will not be joining you for dinner."

"Indeed?" said Mason, completely taken aback. "Is that all he had to say?"

"He also said to tell you that, with deep regrets, the deal is off. That is the full message."

A stunned George Mason sat bolt upright in his chair. To think that he, a top Special Branch agent, had come all this way on a fool's errand. Who the heck was this Hermann Gertler, anyway, and what exactly was his game? The information completely neutralized the sense of euphoria induced by an enjoyable meal. Had all his patient groundwork over the past several weeks come to this? Not if he, George Mason, could help it. The very thought was intolerable, implying as it did an admission of defeat to Chief Inspector Harrington. The waiter, realizing he had conveyed unwelcome news, regarded him with some sympathy as he cleared his plate. The chastened detective skipped dessert, ordered black coffee with brandy and, aware that he had only days left before his recall to London, put his thinking cap back on. He was still there, at his window table, when the last diners were settling their bills and preparing to leave.

chapter 15

GEORGE MASON ROSE early the following morning, enjoyed a warm buffet breakfast in the dining-room, packed his few belongings into his valise and went down to Reception to settle his account. As he did so, a poster in the hotel lobby caught his eye. It was headed SUMMER EVENTS IN TICINO. It listed a series of outdoor concerts, at a lake-side venue, to be presented by the Locarno Symphony; and notices of open-air theater, including *A Midsummer Night's Dream*. Much intrigued, he read on down until his eye fixed on something instantly familiar: 'Annual Pergolesi Festival—*The Maid as Mistress*—Collegio San Isidoro—August 20'. He recalled at once that Meg Fern had strongly recommended it for inclusion in one of his fictitious Bowland Tours. He also recalled that he had seen a similar notice in the doorway of Anton Ziegler's shop. Of the dozens of bookstores he had visited in and around Zurich, only Ziegler's had displayed that particular item. Did that mean the bookseller had a strong interest in early Italian opera? Or did it imply some closer connection with Collegio San Isidoro, possibly as a donor or benefactor? There was only one way to find out.

"How do I get to Collegio San Isidoro?" he asked the hotel clerk.

"Take the post-bus outside the railway station," the clerk replied. "It winds up through the smaller towns and hill villages between Locarno and Bellinzona. The college staff and students use it frequently."

"*Grazie*," the detective said, in his best Italian.

It was a beautiful July day when he stepped out of Hotel Spitz to cover the short distance to the station. A bus trip into the hills, off the beaten tourist track, seemed a useful way to spend the morning and would help offset the sense of disillusion, even betrayal, he had felt on receiving Gertler's curt message. Defeatism was something he would never yield to. What manner of composer was this Pergolesi, he fell to musing as the bus climbed ever higher? Vivaldi and Clementi were fairly familiar to him, from overhearing his wife Adele's CDs. She would be interested to learn what he had discovered about a composer not very well-known in Britain.

The driver set him down at the college gates. It struck Mason as a most impressive campus, with tree-lined walks past well-kept lawns leading up to the main building he thought might once have been a private mansion. Smaller, more modern structures that could have been science blocks or gymnasiums, stood to the right. Beyond those were tennis courts, with games in play. He glimpsed one or two figures in black soutanes and white collars, whom he took to be members of the Aurelian Brothers who ran the school. Obviously a private boarding-school for parents of substantial means, he concluded, as he approached the heavy oaken front door and rang the bell.

After several moments it was opened by an elderly brother with white hair and the benign features of one who had spent most of a long life in a semi-monastic milieu.

"*Buon giorno*," the man said, with an engaging smile. "Can Fra Celestino assist you?"

"*Buon giorno*," Mason returned, eagerly. "I've come to enquire about next month's Pergolesi Festival."

"Are you a musician?" the brother enquired, hopefully. "We are in dire need of a viola player to strengthen the string section."

"Er…no, actually," Mason blustered, feeling sudden qualms about having to tell an untruth to such a spiritual person. A white lie was still a lie. "I represent a British travel company, Bowland Tours. We may wish to include your festival in one of our itineraries."

Fra Celestino's face beamed approval.

"It would be an excellent choice," he said. "The person you must speak to is our Director of Music, Marco Villanuova. Please come this way and I shall introduce you to him."

He opened the door wider, leading the way at a brisk pace across an oak-paneled hall to the adjoining classrooms. He rapped briefly on a door marked Music Department, opened it and ushered the detective inside.

"Your name?" he asked, politely.

"George Mason."

"Marco," he said, addressing the young man sitting behind a large, cluttered desk mounted with a plaster bust of Vivaldi. "This is Signore Mason. He has come all the way from England to enquire about our summer festival."

The music master, much impressed, rose to his feet and proffered his hand.

"Not directly from England," the detective hurriedly explained. "I'm in Switzerland checking out cultural events on behalf of Bowland Tours. A contact in Zurich recommended your Pergolesi Festival. Since I was in the area, in Locarno as a matter of fact, I decided to pay you a quick visit."

Marco Villanuova seemed most gratified. International recognition of his artistic achievements was something he had long hoped for.

"That wouldn't be Jill Crabtree, would it?" he enquired, with a knowing smile.

Mason was a bit taken aback at the knowledge that he knew the American, who was now under police suspicion. Should he let on that he also knew her, he wondered? His instinct told him not to and he shook his head.

"It was a young woman named Margaret Fern," he explained. "I think she attended one of your performances about two years ago."

"Please have a seat," the other said, as Fra Celestino tactfully withdrew, "while I fill you in on the details."

George Mason did as he was bid and listened attentively while the music master gave an account of his current production at some length, even to the extent of explaining difficulties in casting female parts at a school for boys. As he spoke, the detective's attention was caught by a large portrait hanging on the wall behind the music master's desk. When Marco Villanuova had finished his exposition, Mason said:

"That's a fine portrait you have there. Who is it of?"

The music master turned, craning his neck to admire it.

"That's Amadeo d'Alassio," he explained, with evident pride. "He was an officer under Garibaldi in the Risorgimento."

"The Risorgi...?" Mason enquired, struggling with the unfamiliar term.

"The Risorgimento," the other repeated. "The movement towards Italian reunification."

"May I take a closer look?" the detective asked.

"By all means," Marco replied.

George Mason got up and approached the portrait of a dashingly handsome young man in the garb of a nine-teenth-century partisan.

"He was killed at the Battle of Luino," the other explained.

"Where exactly is that?" Mason enquired, vaguely recalling Kubler mentioning it at one of their early meetings, possibly in connection with their investigation.

"On the east bank of Lago di Maggiore," Marco replied.

As he spoke, Mason's gaze wandered from the portrait to the bookshelves below. The title of a handsomely-bound volume immediately caught his eye. It was *The History of Westminster Abbey*. Next to it, to his amazement, was Palladio's *Architettura* in the original Italian; and next to that was Hemingway's *Old Man and the Sea*, with several other titles Leutnant Kubler had mentioned to him. How odd, he thought, recovering from his surprise, that there should be another complete set of those books in addition to the ones Hermann Gertler had offered him. Or *was* it a coincidence, he wondered?

"Very young, isn't he?" he remarked to the music master who, unaware of his visitor's sudden interest in literature, had returned to his task of correcting students' work.

"About thirty-four, I believe. A true patriot."

"Not many of them around, these days," Mason remarked, heading for the door. "Thanks for the information. Much appreciated."

"My pleasure," returned the other, rising to his feet. "Hope to see you before long at one of our performances."

The detective merely nodded, giving no commitment on that score. Once outside, he located Fra Celestino, who was occupied polishing brass altar furnishings in a small storage area just off the hallway. The aged brother interrupted his task and smiled benignly at him.

"Did you get the information you required?" he enquired.

"Absolutely," Mason replied, with heavy emphasis. "And more besides."

Fra Celestino's benign smile gave way to a look of uncertainty, unsure what this untypical visitor to San Isidoro's might be implying.

"Would it be possible for me to make a personal phone call from here?" Mason asked, glad now that Kubler had given him the number of the conference center in case something turned up in his absence.

"By all means," replied Fra Celestino, leading him to the school office at the far end of the hallway. He quickly explained the visitor's needs to the school secretary and as quickly withdrew.

"Do you by any chance have the dialing code for Airolo?" he enquired, thinking from the Italian name that it must be somewhere in Ticino, perhaps not all that far distant.

The secretary, an older woman with tightly-permed gray hair, rose from the computer keyboard, offering to dial the number for him. Within moments, he was speaking with Rolf Kubler.

"*Guten Tag*, Inspector Mason," came the breezy voice of the Swiss officer. "To what do I owe the pleasure?"

"How quickly can you get over here?" Mason asked, imparting urgency to his voice.

"Where, in fact, are you?" Kubler demanded.

"At San Isidoro's, a boys' boarding school in the hills above Bellinzona."

"What on earth are you doing there?"

"I'll explain fully when you get here," Mason replied, with a quick glance towards the secretary. From her composed demeanor back at the computer, he guessed that she did not understand English.

"I know it well," the Swiss said. "My sister's boy recently graduated from there. Luckily for you, our training session has just ended. Give me forty minutes."

"I've quite a surprise in store for you," the detective said, ringing off.

On his way out, he again encountered Fra Celestino in the hallway. The octogenarian gave him a quizzical look, as if not quite sure what to make of him.

"Is there somewhere I can grab a bite to eat?" Mason asked, thinking to fill in time before Rolf Kubler arrived.

"By all means," replied the brother. "Walk down to the main gate and take a right. There's a pizzeria in the village, about a hundred meters down the road. My nephew's son owns it. Tell him Fra Celestino sent you."

"That's very kind of you," Mason said, with feeling. "I'll do that."

"*Buona sera,*" Fra Celestino said, opening the heavy front door to let him out.

"*Arriverderci,*" the detective replied, causing the brother's brows to pucker again in puzzlement. Was this strange Englishman coming back again so soon, he seemed to be wondering?

George Mason set off at a brisk pace towards the village. It was quite cool up here in the hills and the exertion did not trouble him. He would have just sufficient time, he considered, for a small pizza and a glass of wine, so as to be back at the college in time to greet his Swiss colleague.

Anton Ziegler also woke early that morning, as was his wont, and accompanied Hugh Rokeby to breakfast in the dining-room of Hotel Mirafiori, overlooking the broad lake. Following their meal, they walked down to the jetty and boarded the large passenger ship scheduled to depart at nine o'clock on a return voyage to Stresa. As they basked in the early-morning sunshine on the forward deck, the antiquarian bookseller inwardly congratulated himself on the deception he had perpetrated on the unsuspecting and gullible George Mason, whom he fully expected would now be on his way back to Zurich, his tail between his legs.

"I really appreciate your taking time out for a short trip into Italy," the American said, as the vessel slowly pulled away from the quay. "It's a country I've long wanted to visit."

"My pleasure," replied the Swiss, who personally welcomed a break from routine, especially if it helped further his business interests.

"How far to Stresa?" Rokeby asked.

"About an hour," came the reply. "We sail down the west bank, past Cannobio, Cannero Rviera and Verbania."

"Such musical names," the other said. "Freni would have loved to join me, it's so incredibly romantic."

"Then bring her along, why don't you, on your next visit."

"I'm afraid that may be some years away," Rokeby said, with regret. "Have to cover the Far East more and more on upcoming assignments."

"The opportunity will arise," Ziegler assured him, "sooner or later."

They engaged in sporadic conversation, mainly about the book trade, for the duration of the voyage, strolled the decks and had martinis at the bar amidships. The American was much taken by the picturesque towns and villages where the boat, the main mode of transport in the area, briefly called to set down and take on passengers. It was just turned eleven o'clock when, on the return from Stresa, it docked at Luino. The Swiss, agilely for his years, led his American customer down the gangway and at a brisk pace through the busy market town to the railway station, where they caught the stopping train to Bellinzona. It was early afternoon by the time their taxi set them down at the gates of Collegio San Isidoro, from where they covered the short distance on foot to the main entrance.

Fra Celestino answered their summons, opening wide the heavy oaken door. Instead of entering, however, Ziegler immediately drew back in astonishment, as George Mason and Rolf Kubler gingerly crossed the threshold carrying the school computer, which they placed carefully on the rear seat of the lieutenant's car.

"Surprise, surprise, Herr Ziegler," Mason said, turning to the antiquarian. "Or perhaps it's not such a surprise… Herr Gertler?"

Ziegler's features contorted to a look of impotence and rage, that his stratagem had failed. The American looked questioningly at him, expecting quick answers.

"And who might you be, may I ask?" Kubler challenged.

"Hugh Rokeby, a dealer in rare books from Philadelphia. I flew in yesterday morning on perfectly legitimate business."

George Mason raised his eyebrows at that remark and glanced at Kubler.

"I think you had both better accompany me to Airolo police station," Kubler said. "In my possession, I have a selection of books and manuscripts removed from San Isidoro's music department. You both have a deal of explaining to do."

Ziegler said nothing, scowling fiercely at George Mason, who had bested him once again. Hugh Rokeby's face clouded. He looked crestfallen as he squeezed into the rear seat next to the computer. Ziegler occupied the front passenger seat.

"I'd gladly have dropped you off at the station," the lieutenant said to Mason, apologetically. "But there's hardly room."

The look on Kubler's face told the Special Branch man everything. The lieutenant seemed quietly confident that the pieces in this puzzle were finally falling into place. He must already have had suspicions regarding Anton Ziegler, the detective considered, following Erik Muntener's acceptance of a plea bargain. All he needed was hard evidence and he, George Mason, had provided that. What a turn-up, for the two dealers to appear at this critical juncture, fully expecting to do profitable business together. It would trump all other narratives at the Zurich Polizei Dienst for a long time to come.

"When our experts in Airolo have examined the contents of the school computer," Kubler promised him, "I'll be in touch."

The hubbub had drawn onlookers. Fra Celestino stood with two other brothers in black soutanes and a cluster of senior boys, watching the police officer drive off with two mysterious gentlemen and, incredibly, valuable office equipment. What would the principal make of it all, Celestino wondered, when he returned from Rome? Marco Villanuova, totally unaware of events on the forecourt, was busy correcting student exercises in the sanctuary of the music room.

"The next bus to Bellinzona?" Mason asked one of the younger brothers, thinking he would treat himself to a meal at the Wienerwald when he got back to Zurich. Good detective work always sharpened the appetite, and the venue would remind him of the enjoyable fondue evening he had shared with members of the choir.

⊰⊱

Two days later, an upbeat George Mason walked down to the Polizei Dienst at Rolf Kubler's request, the lieutenant being eager to bring him up-to-date on developments resulting from their visit to the Aurelian Brothers' academy. The duty officer, a pert young brunette with an engaging smile, insisted on him signing the visitors' book before showing him in.

"*Guten Morgen*, Inspector," the lieutenant said, in buoyant mood. "Please take a seat."

George Mason returned the greeting and sat facing him, in a mood of keen anticipation. He waited patiently a few moments, while the Swiss shuffled official papers on his desk and replaced them in appropriate files.

"My compliments, Inspector, on a quite remarkable piece of detective work," Kubler began. "I knew we were doing the right thing bringing in Scotland Yard, even though Horst Reinhardt, the cantonal chief of police, was initially skeptical."

"You've arrested Ziegler?"

"Much more than that," Kubler said, beside himself. "We recovered from the computer hard drive a most incriminating file called the Amadeo Agenda."

"What on earth is that?" Mason enquired.

"It *was* a well-advanced plot to stage a military coup against the elected Italian government," the Swiss explained. "You got onto them in the nick of time. It was to take place as early as tomorrow, July 10th. The file, whose full name is Amadeo Agenda Pro Patria Italia, lists the names of the ringleaders, the so-called 'Inner Circle'."

"You amaze me," a dumbfounded Geroge Mason said. "Yet I suspected at an early stage that there was more to all this than mere theft."

"And you were right," Kubler said, in undisguised admiration. "Left to my own devices, I would never have made a connection like that."

"So have we now tied up all the loose ends?" the detective wanted to know.

The lieutenant nodded gravely.

"More or less," he said. "The older Italian gentleman spotted by Kaporal Goetz at the Bellinzona buffet was no less a personage than Count Flavio de Montesedina, an Umbrian vintner with a villa at Stresa. He was one of the key players, second only to *Il Direttore*. In addition, there was a lady professor from San Remo and a businessman named Alessandro Pignatelli. They were all arrested yesterday by the Carabinieri."

"I thought you said it was to be a military coup d'etat?" Mason said.

"I did indeed," Kubler replied. "General Guido Granelli, commanding officer of the 5th Light Infantry, with responsibility for homeland defense, has also been apprehended. His company were to surround the parliament building and arrest the prime minister and leading members of the government. The Alpinisti, crack mountain troops, were to commandeer the television stations ahead of an announcement to the Italian people."

"Give me one guess at the motive," the detective said.

"Go ahead," the Swiss replied, eagerly.

"They were about to install a military dictatorship, take Italy out of the European Union, reintroduce the lira and similar retrograde measures."

"Spot on!" Kubler cried, beside himself. "That, in a nutshell, was precisely their agenda."

"Named after Amadeo d'Alassio," Mason confidently announced. "An officer in the Italian Risorgimento."

"You've been doing your history homework," the lieutenant said, duly impressed. "Risorgimento translates into English as 'rebirth'."

"So they were really aiming for a second rebirth?"

"You could put it like that," Kubler said. "And they might well have succeeded but for your amazing acumen."

George Mason was dismissive of praise.

"All in a day's work," he said, diffidently. "What concerns me most at this stage is the fate of my colleagues in St Wilfrid's choir."

"As we speak, Max Fifield is in another section of this building, awaiting formal charges for receiving stolen goods. He was apparently in cahoots with Anton Ziegler, who will also soon be charged."

"And Jill Crabtree?" a concerned George Mason asked.

"She will face a lesser charge," Kubler explained, "of materially assisting in a money laundering operation. I think, all in all, she was taken advantage of and may, depending on the attitude of the trial judge, be let off with just a caution."

"I sincerely hope so," the detective said, with feeling.

"And, by the way," the Swiss went on, "Interpol have reported back regarding the Hungarian, Laszlo Polke."

"Is his name included in the Amadeo file?" Mason asked, expectantly.

"Actually, no," Kubler replied. "Deposits he made at the Lausanne branch of Balaton Bank were traced to a Tomas Vasaryk, a leading activist in an organization known as Zeged. They have links with other nationalist groups in East Europe, but have no connection with Amadeo."

"Have you arrested him?"

"We shall do, once documentation comes through from Budapest. A clear case of embezzlement, if you ask me."

"Seems to me like an idealist who's stepped over the line," Mason said." A pity, really. Margaret Fern had a soft spot for him, and she's a good judge of character."

"So what is your next move, Inspector?"

"It has little to do with police work," Mason was pleased to assure him. "This coming Whit Sunday at St Wilfrid's, I shall take part in a performance of the Vaughan Williams' anthem we've been rehearsing these past few weeks. With Max Fifield temporarily out of circulation, Dr Hurlimann will be counting on me to steady the basses."

"Perhaps I shall come, and bring my wife. She enjoys choral music."

"By all means, do so," Mason urged, rising to take his leave. "One thing only puzzles me."

"Oh?" enquired the Swiss. "And what is that?"

"You did not reveal the identity of the Amadeo mastermind, or capo, as the Italians would call him."

"I surely did," Rolf Kubler objected. "Didn't I tell you that Count Flavio was second only to *Il Direttore* in the command structure?"

"That tells me very little," Mason retorted.

"*Il Direttore* is the name, in Italian-speaking circles, for the principal of a school. Brother Director might be a good English equivalent."

The penny suddenly dropped for an incredulous George Mason.

"Fra Ignacio!" he exclaimed.

"None other," the lieutenant replied, with a broad grin. "He too is under arrest, much to the consternation of his religious community. The Superior-General of the Aurelian Brothers, a Frenchman named Frere Claude Deschamps, has been summoned urgently to the Vatican. This case will have very wide repercussions, you can be sure of that. Very wide repercussions indeed, at all levels of Italian society. Even beyond."

"You could knock me down with a feather," the Englishman said, with a perverse sort of satisfaction at having opened, however unwittingly, a genuine Pandora's box.

"Kommandant Reinhardt is making representations to Chief Inspector Harrington at Scotland Yard, and to the Italian president, for you to receive special recognition of your outstanding services."

"Just turn up at St Wilfrid's, ten o'clock sharp on Sunday morning," Mason replied, from the office doorway. "That will be recognition and thanks enough for me. I've put in a deal of time and effort at choir rehearsals over the past few weeks."

"*Aufwiedersehen* then, Inspector, rather than *adieu*! And don't forget to tune into the television news this evening. There's to be a special announcement by an Italian government spokesman on all main channels. It could even be the prime minister himself."

"Until Sunday," Mason said, thinking he might do just that and alert Adele in case the announcement was also covered by the BBC. How ironic, and at the same time how satisfying, was his final thought on the matter as he strolled back to his hotel, that it was Anton Ziegler himself who had led him, almost literally, to a solution of the case.

CPSIA information can be obtained
at www.ICGtesting.com
Printed in the USA
BVHW040204300119
539033BV00012B/128/P